COUP

A Murder Mystery in 1870s Paris

by
Paul Bristow

Old Chapel Books, Chislehurst

Published in Great Britain by
Old Chapel Books, Chislehurst,
The Old Chapel, Queens Passage,
Chislehurst, BR7 5AP

Copyright © Paul Bristow
The moral right of Paul Bristow to be identified as the author of this work has been asserted in accordance with the Copyright, Designs and Patents Act of 1988.

All rights reserved. No part of this publication may be reproduced, stored in a retrieval system or transmitted in any form or by any means, electronic, mechanical, photocopying, recording or otherwise, without the prior permission of both the copyright owner and the above publisher of this book.

Published, March 2020

Paperback ISBN: 978-1-912236-17-6

Printed and bound by CPI Group (UK) Ltd, Croydon, CR0 4YY

The front cover includes a painting by Leon Sabatier: 'Paris et ses ruines – Rue de Rivoli – Maisons incendiées le 24 mai 1871', which is part of the collection held by the Museums of the City of Paris.

To Anne

Contents

Historical Note	vii
Note on Characters	ix
Chapter One – Sunday 28 May 1871 – Paris	1
Chapter Two – Friday 9 June – Paris	9
Chapter Three – Tuesday 13 June – Paris	17
Chapter Four – Tuesday 13 June – Montmartre Cemetery	25
Chapter Five – Tuesday 13 June – Rue de Rotterdam	33
Chapter Six – Tuesday 13 June – Pension Frensham	39
Chapter Seven – Wednesday 14 June – Pension Frensham	45
Chapter Eight – Thursday 15 June – London	51
Chapter Nine – Thursday 15 June – Paris	55
Chapter Ten – Friday 16 June – Paris	59
Chapter Eleven – Friday 16 June – Pension Frensham	65
Chapter Twelve – Friday 16 June – Rue du Delta	69
Chapter Thirteen – Friday 16 June – Impasse des Vieux Arbres	77
Chapter Fourteen – Saturday 17 June – Caserne de la Cité	81
Chapter Fifteen – Monday 19 June – London	87

Historical Note

In 1852, the French Second Empire was ushered in by Napoléon III (nephew of Napoléon Bonaparte); it lasted 18 years. But in July 1870, France opened a war against Prussia which it lost by the end of August of the same year. Napoléon III relinquished power and fled to England, to spend the last years of his life in Chislehurst. The Third Republic was proclaimed in France.

While the rest of the country yielded to Prussia, Paris held out. The city was subjected to a siege which lasted 130 days and ended in January 1871 only after a three-week bombardment and near-starvation for many Parisians. A general election was held. Adolphe Thiers, a veteran politician aged 73, emerged as the head of the national government, and moved quickly to conclude a peace treaty with Prussia (that involved France's loss of Alsace and Lorraine).

Even as matters were settled with the foreign foe, however, the national government was confronted by the "enemy within". Political turmoil in Paris allowed radical elements to gain control of the city and set up the Paris Commune at the end of March 1871. The Commune's words and deeds threatened a return to the terror of the French Revolution of 1789. Leaders of the Commune ordered the taking of hostages, including the Archbishop of Paris; and there was fighting between the National Guard, loyal to the Commune, and the armed forces of the national government, now based in Versailles.

In May 1871, the Versailles government's troops attacked Paris, taking three weeks to drive the National Guard back across the city to final defeat. There was savagery on both sides, which included the summary execution of the Archbishop and other clergy. It culminated in the bloody week – "la semaine sanglante" – at the end of May, when as many as 20,000 people died on the streets of Paris, and some of the city's finest buildings were torched and burnt to the ground.

Denunciations, arrests and reprisal killings continued for weeks after the collapse of the Commune. In June 1871, even as bars, restaurants and theatres re-opened, and Thomas Cook offered British visitors tours to see the ruins of Paris, the hunt for the Communards went on, out of sight of the public. The Third Republic had a 70-year life, ending in 1940, but it was born out of the cruelties of a civil war.

Note on Characters

(All characters, except Thiers, are fictitious creations)

Lucien de BOIZILLAC: born in 1820, to a family of notables in rural France, Boizillac entered the Army and served in Algeria from 1841 to 1849. After leaving military service, he became a captain in the Paris police force, and took on several murder investigations in the early 1850s (narrated in *Coup de Tête, Coup de Pierre* and *Coup de Guerre*). In the late 1860s, he steps back from the front line into administration.

Laure de BOIZILLAC (née Carreleur): born in 1830, and raised from the age of three by her older brother Marc after her mother and siblings died of cholera. After a career as an actress, Laure married Lucien in 1854. They have a son, Marc-Antoine, born in 1855.

Marc CARRELEUR: born in 1823, older brother to Laure, Marc also served in the French Army in Algeria, returning to civilian life in 1847. After initially resisting the regime of Napoléon III, Marc became an informer on remaining dissidents. From the early 1850s onwards, he makes his money working on the construction of the new Paris of the Second Empire.

Octavius LUKER: born in 1811, founder and head of the firm of Luker, Ledouin and Stytche, Investigation Agents (based at 13 Bethnal Green Cut in London). Unwittingly involved in the murders unravelled by Boizillac in 1852, Luker speaks French well and has a good knowledge of Paris.

Georges TISSERAND: born in 1836, an artist who flees Paris in May 1871 and comes to London.

Camille NOIRET: born in 1840, Tisserand's lover who remains in Paris.

Joséphine ROLLIN: born in 1845, a friend of Camille Noiret and fellow supporter of the Commune.

Emmanuel SIMON: born in 1842, a former soldier who joins the Paris Police in 1871 and operates alongside Boizillac.

Lewis MARDON: an English house agent, working in Paris.

Sophia SCALES: an Englishwoman running a pension in Paris. Both

Lewis Mardon and Sophia Scales appear in "The Old Wives' Tale" by Arnold Bennett.

Adolphe THIERS: born in 1797, a key figure in the revolutions in France in 1830 (which ended the Bourbon monarchy under Charles X) and in 1848 (which ended the Orléans monarchy under Louis-Philippe). A prominent critic of Napoléon III, he becomes head of the national government in 1871 and oversees the suppression of the Paris Commune.

Chapter One
Sunday 28 May 1871
Paris

For four days, Paris had been burning, the air thick with smoke and cinders. The Tuileries, the Prefecture of Police, the Hôtel de Ville, all were consumed by flames started by the shells aimed at the Commune by the troops of the Versailles Government – or lit by the Communards themselves. If they were to perish at the end of this bloody week, they wanted first to destroy the strongholds of reaction.

As he watched the fires, Marc Carreleur knew that his own hopes were ended. For more than fifteen years, he had made a career across the building sites that appeared in Paris during the Second Empire of Napoléon III. The jumbled clutter of centuries-old houses and streets was swept away for the new boulevards of Baron Haussmann; and Carreleur was one of the gang-masters controlling the brick-layers and masons who raised up the five-storey mansions that ranged along the new thoroughfares.

Then, nine months before, the Emperor and his Army were humiliated in the war against Prussia. The country surrendered; only Paris held out, and was besieged until its nerve finally broke in January. Carreleur stayed in the city, even as many of his fellow citizens fled to the provinces. He had lived here all his life, nearly five decades; he had no wish to go elsewhere.

In March, the Commune took control of Paris, and spat in the face of the National Government that the Prussians had allowed to sit in Versailles. For a moment, it seemed that the common man, and woman, might at last come into their rights; the city would be their protector, rather than their oppressor.

Carreleur had rallied to the Commune. Before he had become a house-builder, before his hair, his coats and his boots were chalked with the dust of the construction sites, he was a passionate republican, an agitator against the onset of the Empire. When Napoléon III seized power in 1851, Carreleur avoided imprisonment only by turning informer against his former co-conspirators. He had closed his mind to the shame that this betrayal caused him. Now there was a chance to redeem himself.

Others spent their days debating the future direction of the Commune, or making speeches to gatherings of adherents. Carreleur gave practical support, helping to to strengthen the defences of the capital or repair houses damaged by the bombardment which the Versailles Government unleashed on the city in April.

The Government's troops had fought their way into the city a week before. But it was only on 24 May, when fire incinerated the landmark buildings in the centre, that Carreleur's hopes failed. Ash was death: the life of a city was its buildings.

And now death stalked the streets. Two days before, a fanatical group of Communards butchered a mixed group of *gendarmes* and priests, 50 men who had been held as hostages for over a month. Today Carreleur had heard that the Versailles troops had taken 150 Communards to the cemetery at Père Lachaise and shot them all dead. The same fate threatened anyone who was known to have helped the Commune, or even suspected of doing so.

Carreleur would not give himself up to that fate. His heart may have ruled his head when he threw in his lot with the Commune in March, but his mind was clear enough now: he had no wish to share in its end. He knew the city better than most. If he could not escape, he would find some cleft in its fabric where he could hide.

* * *

Thursday 8 June
London

It was a slow morning in the offices of Luker, Ledouin and Stytche, Investigation Agents. Octavius Luker had arrived at 13 Bethnal Green Cut at his habitual starting-time of half past seven, and climbed the stairs, ignoring the stiffness in his limbs which grew more troublesome as the months went by. Three more months, and he would have completed six decades on this Earth. As he unlocked the door to his offices, he silently congratulated himself on the decision he had made some years before, to move his agency down from the third and topmost storey of the building to the first floor. "Only four-and-twenty steps now," he thought. "More than enough for a veteran like me. To think – I used to scale three times as many!"

At the same time as his business descended nearer to street level, Luker had taken on a younger partner, Percival Stytche (Olivier Ledouin had always been Luker's shadow alter ego, a name without a body, adopted to give weight to the agency's title). Stytche was a member of the Metropolitan Police until a misunderstanding with his superiors (over his liking for the "alcoholic offerings of divers tenebrous taverns", as the reproving phrase went) led to his resignation. When Stytche was sober, he had a talent for investigation work which Luker found invaluable. Though beer and wine still called out to the younger man, he had never missed more than one working day in five as a result. His success during the rest of the week more than compensated for these occasional absences.

Whether Stytche would be at his desk today was a moot point. The previous evening he had told Luker that he was going to meet some of his former police colleagues at the Green Dragon inn, in Bishopsgate. They both knew that he would soak up at least as much information as alcohol, but also that he might very well need more than one night's sleep to absorb both.

Luker settled himself at his own desk. To an unschooled observer, the absence of letters, bills or folders might suggest that the agency had little in hand; but its principal prided himself on the confidentiality of its operations, which meant that nothing should be left out where it might be seen and read by a third party. There were indeed careful records of past investigations; if in paper form, they were secured in one of the rooms at the back of the office suite; but there was a second store of detail, of names and of findings, held inside Luker's head. Though his hair had thinned and become grey, his memory was unfaded.

And it was his memory that kept him company as the morning wore on. Percival Stytche did not appear. Luker had a handful of letters to write to clients whose cases were still underway but, as he rested his pen, his thoughts went back over the many investigations he had completed. Each had held its own interest for him, bringing him ever new insights into the misdeeds of his fellow men and women, their impulses and their suspicions. He still relished the challenges of his work but, though the spirit was always willing, the flesh was often weak. His head dropped forward a little. Perhaps the time was approaching when he should hand the agency over to Stytche, lock, stock and barrel. Perhaps the time...

The office clock chimed eleven. "The time!" Luker was jolted from the sleep that had crept over him. At that moment there was a knock at the door. Shaking off his torpor, he stood up from his chair and went to admit the visitor. It was a man in his thirties, wearing a black frock-coat that had seen better days; he carried a large portfolio case. A full black beard heightened the pallor of his face. "Are you Mister Luker?" The voice was accented.

"Octavius Luker at your service. Please, come in." He ushered the visitor to a chair, shut the door, and sat down again. "May I know your name?"

"I am Georges Tisserand."

"You are French?"

Tisserand nodded. "*Mon pauvre pays.* Like so many of my compatriots, I have left my home to seek a better life in England."

"*Si vous voulez, Monsieur Tisserand, nous pouvons parler en français.*" It was not for nothing that Luker had devised a French second persona, in the form of Olivier Ledouin. He had a fluency that had served him well in some of his investigations.

Tisserand smiled briefly, but his expression quickly regained its initial seriousness. "Thank you, but I wish to persevere with the language of the country that I have now adopted. But I know of your ability to speak French. That is one reason why I wish to consult you." Luker gave him a questioning look. "Auguste Rolandin told me about you. I believe that you have assisted him?"

The other man recognised the name at once. Rolandin had established a thriving art dealership in Paris during the Second Empire, only to move himself, his family and his stock to London the previous autumn in the wake of the Franco-Prussian War. By Christmas, his eighteen-year-old daughter had contrived to fall in love with yet another exile from France; Rolandin *père* retained Luker to look into the background of the suitor and was grateful for his report exonerating the young man of any untoward traits (if slightly disappointed by the outcome).

"I hope that I was of service to Monsieur Rolandin."

"He has been good enough to help me settle in London. I am a painter, and Auguste sold several of my works in the last few years. I contacted him when I left Paris, a week ago. You know what has happened there?"

"I have read disturbing reports in our newspapers. There has been fighting between the forces of the Government in Versailles and the adherents of the Commune, as I believe it is called, with widespread destruction in the capital. It seems that a great misfortune has befallen the City of Light."

"A great misfortune, yes indeed. Many have fallen in the battles in the streets – and many more have been captured and then executed, shot dead like mad dogs."

"Were you a witness to these events?"

Tisserand placed on the table the portfolio case that he had carried, and opened it. There were several pencil sketches. They showed a tall brick wall rising up above some rough ground: a dozen bodies lay, twisted and broken at the base of the wall; a single human form was caught in mid-air, head shattered by gunshot, tumbling towards the corpses below.

After waiting while Luker looked over the drawings, Tisserand spoke: "This was what I saw, only ten days ago, in the last days of May. These are some of National Guards who fought for the Commune and were captured by the Versailles forces. They were taken to the fortifications at the Bois de Boulogne, shot at point-blank range, and thrown into the ditch like unwanted scraps of meat." He pressed his hand against his mouth, then went on: "While I watched, I saw fifty or more of these executions. But I know that this scene was repeated time and time again across Paris. Thousands have died, Mister Luker, thousands."

"I am saddened to hear it. I too would have found it troublesome to stay in a city where such deeds were done."

"Let me be honest with you, Mister Luker. It was not simply the horror of these scenes that drove me away. The Commune may have lasted for little more than two months, but for me and for others it held great promise of finally realising freedom, equality and fraternity. I gave it my support, all too publicly. And for that I have become an enemy of the state that has now been established under Monsieur Thiers. That is why I left Paris when I did."

"And if you had stayed?"

Tisserand's eyes blazed for a second, and there was bitterness in his voice when he spoke. "Gustave Courbet stayed. Courbet, who painted the stone-breakers, and the peasants of Flagey, and so many more masterpieces." The paintings were unknown to Luker, but he nodded complaisantly. "You know that he has now been seized, and will be tried for insurrection, because he championed the Commune? I stood alongside Courbet, in his work for the Federation of Artists. If I had stayed, at best I would have been arrested as well. At worst, I would have been shot and thrown into an unmarked grave. So I fled Paris as soon as it was possible for me to do so. I brought with me little more than these sketches – and this portrait."

He carefully removed a small canvas from the portfolio. It showed the face of a woman. "Camille." He could say no more for some moments.

"It is a charming portrait, Monsieur Tisserand." The beauty of youth was apparent in the woman's face, a fresh complexion framed by a swirling mass of deep brown hair. Most striking were the eyes, also brown, and returning the onlooker's gaze with a force that was challenging and inviting at the same time. If the painter's technique, of stippling the oil paint in a fine mosaic of touches, gave Luker pause, he made no comment on it.

Tisserand spoke again. "Camille Noiret. The love of my life." His voice was strained. "I had hoped that she would travel with me to London. But she chose to stay in Paris, to be near her father, a widower, and an old man. She chose to face the hazards that I have escaped."

"You mean the fighting that has taken place in the city?"

"No, Mister Luker, I mean the risk of persecution by the Versailles Government. Camille was also a supporter of the Commune. I fear for her safety, but...I cannot return in present circumstances."

"And have you no way of communicating with her?"

"No. I dare not write to her, in case my letter falls into the wrong hands." He leaned towards Luker. "You have seen her portrait. Do you think that you would recognise her if you met her?"

The investigation agent studied the painting again. "I am sure that I would."

"Then...can I ask you to go to Paris and find her for me? I would of course pay you for such a mission."

It took Luker several seconds to reply. He had visited Paris a number of times over the years in the furtherance of his investigations; and, though he enjoyed the atmosphere of the city, each trip triggered the neuralgic memory of his first visit there, twenty years before, and of his inadvertent complicity in the death of Louis Rougemont, of much the same age then as Georges Tisserand was now. It was not by his hand, nor through his intention, that Rougemont had perished; but Luker had employed Rougemont in a process of deception that had placed the young man in the way of harm.

"Mister Luker?" The Frenchman's voice broke in upon the agent's recollection.

"Monsieur Tisserand, I apologise for my momentary distraction."

"Are you reluctant to go to Paris because of the disorder there?"

"By no means." Luker spoke now with resolve. "I have no concerns on that score. I cannot imagine that the Versailles Government would have any interest, hostile or otherwise, in an insignificant Englishman in the twilight of his years. I shall be pleased to act on your behalf."

Tisserand got up and shook the other man's hand. "Merci, mon ami. How soon can you go?"

"As to that, I must first speak to my partner, Percival Stytche. I expect to be able to do so tomorrow. He is otherwise engaged today. However, barring unforeseen difficulties, I would hope to leave for Paris at the end of this week."

Chapter Two
Friday 9 June
Paris

Lucien de Boizillac was back in the city where he had lived for over twenty years. Like almost all his colleagues in the Paris police, he had quit the capital in mid-March, when the bloody failure of troops to recapture cannon seized by the working-class militia of the National Guard precipitated the Government's departure to Versailles. Two of the troops' commanding officers had been seized and brutally killed by the mob. The Commune took over the running of the city; there was no place for the police, seen as the lackeys of the despised establishment.

Lucien took his wife and son to the house in Châteauroux, 150 miles south of the capital, where he had grown up. Only his mother, now in her ninth decade, still lived there, with a handful of servants; and, though she had not approved of Lucien's marrying Laure, an actress, in 1854, she overcame her earlier hostility, and welcomed the fugitives with open arms. Against expectation, their stay went well; and, as news reached them of the ongoing death and destruction in Paris, the walls of the old family home felt even more protective.

Laure and Marc-Antoine remained in Châteauroux when Lucien answered the call to return to his duties. After a day-long journey, he went first to the apartment in the Boulevard d'Inkermann, in Neuilly, which they had locked in haste when they left in March. By good fortune, it was intact – even though buildings all around had been laid waste by the shells fired into Neuilly when Government forces bombarded the city in April. Houses constructed only a few years before had been battered to the ground. Streets were still disfigured by blocks of masonry blasted from crumbling walls; the wind whipped up eddies of plaster and brick dust that stung the faces of pedestrians and left them rubbing their eyes. Lucien decided that it would be better for his wife and son to stay a while longer in their provincial refuge.

For the last five years, he had worked in an office at the Prefecture, overseeing the activities of the Sûreté, the detective arm of the Paris police. In the fifteen years before that, he was one of the Sûreté's agents, running to ground the murderers and larcenists whose crimes cast shadows across the City of Light. His partner throughout was Daniel Delourcq, an older man who had joined the police force after an apprenticeship in petty crime (unlike Lucien, who came from a military background). Delourcq dressed and spoke like the villains they brought to justice, and Lucien had relied unthinkingly on the other man's street knowledge. When a week's bitterly cold weather settled inside Delourcq's lungs and ended his life in the winter of 1865, Lucien lost his appetite for the investigative work that had taken the two of them to the darker places of the city. He was only too happy to spend his days in the Prefecture's offices, helping to direct the agents who sought to contain the evils of the Second Empire's underworld.

But, for the moment, all that had changed again. The old Prefecture building was in ruins, gutted by one of the many fires that had combined in the Commune's funeral pyre. Though the Government had returned to the city from Versailles, so much of its former accommodation was destroyed that Ministers and officials were forced into temporary lodgings, in banks, commerce-houses, even hotels. Space was found for the police in the barrack block – the Caserne de la Cité – that had been built some ten years before in the heart of the metropolis.

Lucien could have laid claim to a desk in one of its cramped boltholes. He chose otherwise. After the chaos of the past two months, there was an urgent need for the police to re-assert their presence on the streets. The army had summarily executed hundreds of the insurgents, and marched thousands more off to detainment camps outside the city. But there was little doubt in the minds of Government leaders that many had slipped through the net. They had to be found.

It was work that Lucien had done before, in his first years in the Paris police, when Louis-Napoléon – Napoléon III – and his supporters had seized power and ordered a man-hunt, to capture and imprison those who resisted the new imperial regime. Though the work had been as distasteful to him then as it was now, Lucien knew that it was inevitable – and he felt that his experience equipped him to carry out the mission both effectively and humanely.

And there was a personal reason for him to get back out on to the streets. Laure had a brother, Marc Carreleur, who stayed in Paris during the turmoil of the Commune. She'd had no word from him for several months. Lucien was uneasy about the path that he might have followed in that time; tracing the footsteps of the Communards could help him discover what had become of his brother-in-law.

※ ※ ※

Monday 12 June
Paris – Pension Frensham, Rue Lord Byron

Luker sat quietly at breakfast. Percival Stytche had not let him down. He was back in the office only a short time after Luker himself arrived there the previous Friday. The hints and whispers that he had heard in the Green Dragon more than justified his absence the day before; and he was in no way discountenanced by Luker's intention to travel to France in search of Camille Noiret.

"Artist's muse, is she, Mister Luker? I don't know much about such matters, but I'd hazard that an artist who's lost his muse is about as flummoxed as a dog that's lost its bone. I'm sure that, if anyone can dig her out, you can, Mister Luker. So you take yourself off to Paris and dig, dig, dig! I'll take good care of the agency while you're away."

Stytche had proved himself before. If any new clients presented themselves, he would handle them well: less ingratiatingly than Luker, but with a quiet confidence that was undoubtedly reassuring. And while the cat was away, the mouse didn't play: further visits to the Green Dragon inn would be put off until the older man returned.

It was not the first time that he had stayed at the Pension, run by the Frenshams who, despite their name, were English. But there was an unfamiliar air of neglect about the place. Always before, the dining-room had been full of his compatriots, talking loudly about the strange, puzzling and sometimes titivating sights they had encountered in this alien metropolis. Today there was only a handful of other guests scattered across the room. The radiance of Paris had faded and dimmed, and left the Pension Frensham in a fretful gloom.

His journey, undertaken over the weekend, had given him a foretaste of what he would find. He had taken the sea-packet that fought its way from Dover to Calais late on Saturday, and then the train that bounced and clattered through the night to arrive in Paris on Sunday morning. Luker was a seasoned traveller: the sea-crossing dulled his senses, but failed to disturb his stomach; and, while the train's progress through darkness offered little mental stimulus, it was a good deal more comfortable. Wrapped in his well-worn greatcoat, Luker slept for most of the distance.

It was all the more restful since he was alone in his compartment; and, so far as he could judge as he disembarked from the boat and scurried to the train, there were very few other passengers. He had made the same late-night journey before, and was used to encountering parties of over-excited Englishmen and women, chattering and laughing all the way to Paris. Not this time. The reports of death and destruction that crossed the Channel had stopped the flow of visitors. It was an ill wind that brought no good to anyone; in bringing the news of disaster to England, it meant that, apart from the rattle of the wheels on the rail-tracks, the train at least was unusually peaceful.

The maid came to his table. "Have you finished your egg, sir?"

He smiled and nodded. Gone were the days when he had appetite at the start of the day for a plate heaving with ham and other meats; a boiled egg was enough for him. "But bring me some more coffee, would you?" He had been relieved to find that the coffee served by the Frenshams was as tasty as ever and, it seemed to him, far better than anything he drank in London. It always served to put a better spring into his step.

And he needed a fillip after the previous day. Perhaps he could have used it better; but, after leaving his cases at the Pension, he had spent Sunday strolling slowly along the streets, seeing for himself the scars left by the last months. The stump of the column to victory that had been toppled and smashed by the revolutionaries stuck out of the ground in the Place Vendôme like a mutilated arm. The empty archways and windows of the shattered Hôtel de Ville gaped like bruised mouths and empty eye-sockets. The Tuileries Palace, where the deposed Emperor had once held glittering balls and sumptuous dinners, was now a shell of smoke-blackened walls, ripped open and left exposed to wind and rain. No wonder so many had fled the city.

The maid refilled his cup. As he took his first mouthful, one of the other guests, who had just finished his breakfast at another table, came over. He was a younger man, dressed in an indifferent suit which fitted closely around his rather flabby arms and waist. "May I introduce myself? Lewis Mardon. Might I join you for a moment?" He smiled, enthusiastically.

Luker was not keen to have his thoughts interrupted, but he had no good reason to brush Mardon's approach off. "Of course. My name is Octavius Luker."

"Very pleased to make your acquaintance, Mister Luker." Mardon lowered himself on to a chair. "Are you making an extended stay here?"

"That remains to be seen. A few days, at all events. And you, sir?"

Mardon leaned forward, tapped his nose, and beamed. "If my business prospers, I may remain for an indeterminate period." He sat back. "No doubt, Mister Luker, you will wish to know what that business is. I am a house agent, sir. If you wish to settle in Paris, I'm your man."

"Indeed? Would I be wrong, then, in thinking that in its present condition the city can attract few prospective settlers?"

"I follow your reasoning entirely, sir. But I have no doubt that in a year, or sooner, the city will regain its former allure, and our fellow countrymen will rediscover their taste for la vie parisienne. I am seeking to invest a modest amount of capital in one or two properties which now stand neglected, so as to be able to respond in the months ahead to the demand for pieds à terre which I expect to arise."

"Well, well. Much as I cherish Paris, Mister Mardon, I have no plans to acquire a property here."

"May I inquire as to the purpose of your visit?"

Even before leaving London, Luker had fashioned a story to tell in such circumstances, an account which explained his journey without disclosing his real purpose. "I have an elderly relative here. My family has lost communication with him, and I have offered to try and discover what has become of him."

Mardon's face momentarily took on a more serious look. "I wish you every success, sir. I trust that your relative will not have suffered overly from the privations of the last months. I have some knowledge of the city and its present state. Might I ask in which area your relative resides?"

"Do you know of the Rue du Delta? It is at the northern end of the second arrondissement."

"But that is near Montmartre, surely?" The other man nodded. "I would not wish to cause you undue concern, Mister Luker, but

Montmartre was the scene of some of the fiercest fighting in recent weeks." Tisserand had said as much when they had talked the previous week. "Are you content to carry out your quest alone? I would be willing to put my business aside for a day to assist you."

This was the last thing that Luker wanted. He adopted a pained tone. "I know that I am of considerably more advanced years than yourself, Mister Mardon, but I still trust myself to find my way through a city that is not unknown to me."

Mardon raised his hands in apology. "Forgive me, sir, I meant no slight on your age. My only thought was that, in the present circumstances, where destruction and disorder are widespread..."

Luker interrupted him. "I do not begrudge your solicitude, Mister Mardon. But I have no wish to impose upon you. I have already seen some of the damage that has been done to Paris. I know to tread carefully when I look for my relative." He drained his cup, and set down on the table the napkin that he used to dab his mouth. "I should delay my search no longer."

Mardon stood up. "Allow me to wish you well, Mister Luker. I hope that we may converse again before you depart."

The other man got up as well, and smiled briefly, without offering a response. They left the dining-room and parted company.

When Luker emerged from the hotel half an hour later and hailed a cab, he had in his mind's eye the face of Camille Noiret that he had seen in the portrait in London. She might be any one of the women that he passed in the streets, her features disguised to avoid recognition, but it was pointless to try and scan the passers-by for some familiar aspect. He must approach his search systematically, starting at her house.

The Rue du Delta surprised him. It had escaped both the transformation imposed on so many parts of Paris by Baron Haussmann, and the fractures and pockmarks that had been left by the fighting of recent times. Modest villas rubbed shoulders with one another. The building to which Tisserand had directed him had a low wall enclosing a small area of garden at the front; a gate gave on to a short path, leading to a two-storey house that would not have looked out of place in the countryside around Versailles.

Luker could see that the shutters on the windows were closed. He went through the gate and knocked on the front door. Somewhere above his head a couple of pigeons fluttered into the air, but there was no other response. He waited for a minute or two, and then knocked again.

"You're wasting your time." He turned towards the speaker, a man he judged to be of about his age, who stood at the other side of the gate. "There's no-one in the house."

Luker walked to the gate. "I was looking for Jean-Pierre Noiret. I am a relative of his, from England."

"You have travelled from England to see him?"

"Yes. The family has heard nothing from him for months."

"I see. Your name, monsieur?"

"Octavius Luker."

"You speak very good French, Mister Luker. I am Théodore Claudel, a neighbour and friend of your relative." He stepped into the garden, a walking-stick in his left hand, and rested his right hand on Luker's shoulder. "I am sorry to tell you that Jean-Pierre passed away only two or three days ago. He had been ill for some time. The house is empty."

Luker forced himself to wait for some seconds, and to speak in the same hushed tones as the other man: "May he rest in peace." Then: "And his daughter? Was she not living here as well? What has become of her?"

"Camille? She stayed with her father until the last. But when he died, she closed everything up and left." Claudel kept his eyes on the ground, and poked at a weed with his stick. "I cannot say where she has gone."

"Has Jean-Pierre's funeral taken place?"

"No, he is to be buried tomorrow, in the Montmartre cemetery."

"I see. Surely his daughter will be there?"

"I cannot say," Claudel repeated. "I fear that, in these troubled times, there will be few enough mourners to see Jean-Pierre committed to the soil."

"But you will be there?" The other man nodded. "Well, I trust that it will be acceptable if I also attend, to pay my respects – and, I hope, to see Camille."

Claudel paused, then said: "This cannot be what you expected to find when you left England."

"I had hoped that Jean-Pierre would still be with us, certainly –

but the long silence had filled me with apprehension, I must admit." He paused. "But in this life, all of us walk through the valley of the shadow of death."

"And we are told to fear no evil, Mister Luker."

They were silent for a few seconds. Luker spoke again. "What time is the funeral tomorrow?"

Claudel shaded his eyes. "Come to the Montmartre cemetery at noon."

Luker shook his hand. "Thank you for your help, Monsieur Claudel. I shall see you tomorrow." Leaving the other man in the garden, Luker went through the gate and walked towards the Rue de Rochechouart, to find a cab.

Chapter Three
Tuesday 13 June
Paris

Boizillac knew only too well that Judas Iscariot had many descendants among the citizens of Paris. Over twenty years, he had lost track of the number of times that furtive-looking concierges had taken him by the elbow and whispered a warning to him about someone living at their address, or street-traders had squealed on one of their number for selling stolen goods. As often as not, the tip-offs were motivated by personal feuds; but sometimes they helped him, and other agents, to discover real villains, and bring them to justice. The art was to separate the wheat from the chaff.

Within a day or two of the police settling into the Caserne de la Cité, the letters of denunciation flowed in. Of course, some of the individuals named in them were guilty of nothing more than annoying the letter-writer. But the Government wanted no stone to be left unturned, and no Communard to escape retribution. All the denunciations were to be followed up. What was wheat, and what was chaff, would emerge in due course.

A daily routine had established itself. Boizillac, and the other manhunters, would meet at the start of the day and sift through the latest harvest of letters. As far as was possible from any address given, they were sorted on a geographical basis, and teams of two or more would spread out across the city to follow up the leads and try to flush out the Government's opponents.

Boizillac had spent Monday scouring the docks at La Villette. Many of the warehouses which stored the cargo transported along the canal had been destroyed as the army closed in on the last strongholds of the Commune. Work was already underway to clear away the debris at the southern end of the docks; the city needed all its supply routes to be open again, and the canal was no exception. But there had been a written denunciation claiming that the shamble of buildings at the northern end served as a hiding-place for one or more of the insurrectionists.

After a brief consultation with the dockmaster, a taciturn man who grumbled his doubts about the success of the quest, Boizillac and the sergent de ville who accompanied him picked their way through the broken doorways, shattered storerooms and crumbling halls that had not yet been tackled by the clean-up. There were cellars to be checked as well; and, where fallen masonry fouled the access, Boizillac prevailed upon the dockmaster to lend him a couple of workers to move it. It was a slow process. Food waste in one of the cellars showed that someone had made use of it, but then gone, perhaps a week before, or longer.

By the end of the afternoon they had completed a thorough search, but it yielded nothing more than some chicken bones and vegetable scraps, and a lungful of dust. The day left him with mixed feelings: disappointment that their efforts had not unearthed a renegade in hiding; also, illogically, relief that they had not been required to seize anyone and hand them over to the rigours of Army detention; and a fatalistic feeling that the same pattern would be repeated in the weeks to come.

But Tuesday brought a surprise. When Boizillac reported for duty, there was an unfamiliar face in the building. Emmanuel Simon was in his late twenties, much the same age as Boizillac had been when he joined the Sûreté. There was little remarkable about him, save for the overly long and bushy moustache which helped to age his appearance, and the bandaging which could be seen around his neck, above the collar of his shirt.

"Captain de Boizillac?" It had been some time since he was addressed with his former military rank; he nodded. "I am Sub-Lieutenant Emmanuel Simon." He saluted.

Boizillac returned the greeting. "Are you still serving, Simon?"

"No longer. I have left the Army to join the Paris police, and I have the honour to be assigned to work with you." He handed him a letter, dated the previous day, and signed by the Prefect himself, which confirmed Simon's words.

A minute or so passed while Boizillac read the letter, and reflected on this turn of events. Working with the sergents de ville was straightforward; they followed his orders, and were the brawn to his brain. But Simon would bring a second mind to operations, and one that had no knowledge of police work. He would complicate matters, no doubt. Still, Boizillac had himself been a novice two decades before, and Delourcq, God rest his soul, had put up with his inexperience until they found a way to rub along together.

"I am glad of your company, Simon." He gave him back the letter. "And where did you serve?"

"I was in Bourbaki's Army, and fought at the Lizaine in the East. After we were released from internment in Switzerland, I joined the forces at Versailles that reclaimed the city from the Commune."

"The last few months have been hard for you."

Simon shrugged. "And for France. Bad enough that so many were killed in the war against the Prussians. That even more fell in the fight for Paris – well, to use the mot de Cambronne, that was pure shit. Excuse the language of the barrack-room, sir."

It was a sentiment that Boizillac had heard from others, and was not surprising in the mouth of someone who had been in the conflict. "Were you wounded in the fighting?" he asked.

"Shot in the leg at the Lizaine, but not serious."

"And this?" Boizillac pointed at Simon's bandaged neck.

The other man flinched briefly. "A burn, from a spar that fell on me when we fighting near the Hôtel de Ville. Over two weeks ago. It's healing, but slowly."

"We have long days here, Simon. Will this burn hinder you?"

"No, sir. If it weren't for the bandage, you wouldn't notice any difference between me and anyone else."

"You know the work we're doing here." Simon nodded. "I spent yesterday at La Villette, and it looks like I'll be heading back there today. This letter is from the concierge of one of the houses on the Rue de Rotterdam. It's only a stone's throw from the dock-basin. She thinks that a couple in the rooms on the top floor were Communards."

"Rue de Rotterdam?" Simon's voice took on an edge, and his face flushed.

"Do you know it?"

"La Villette, and the streets around it, was one of the last engagements I took part in with the Army. I thought we flushed all the revolutionary scum out."

"Perhaps you did," Boizillac replied, more calmly. "Perhaps the concierge – Bernadette Dubois – is letting her imagination run away with her. She wouldn't be the first. But she claims to have overheard incriminating conversations between the couple. We need to investigate her claims. Are you ready to go?"

The younger man looked nonplussed for a second or two, then stood to attention. "I'm ready, sir."

"Very good, Simon." Boizillac folded up the letter and put it in the pocket of his coat. "I appreciate your military background, Simon, but this is no longer the Army. You're not on parade here." He smiled briefly. "Now, let's find a cab."

It took half an hour for them to reach Rue de Rotterdam, under darkening skies. Though Simon maintained a silence when they first settled into the cab, Boizillac wanted to know more about his background. The Battle of the Lizaine, fought in the depths of the winter, had been a humiliation for the French Army. Simon had been one of 140,000 French soldiers whose attacks had been held off by a Prussian force of only some 50,000 men. "So you saw action at the Lizaine?"

"That was my first real battle." He glanced at Boizillac. "You know how it was. The Prussians had dug themselves in all along the other side of the river. We threw ourselves at them time after time. I was part of the attack at Héricourt – that was where I got shot in the leg."

"But there was no breakthrough?"

"The bloody Prussians stuck to their positions like limpets to rocks. After three days, Bourbaki ordered a retreat." He glanced out of the cab. "That was the worst part of it. It had been cold before, but we'd been fighting, and our blood was up. Now we were just running away, with next to no rations, bivouacking on snow and ice, with our boots frozen to our legs. After ten days of it, we crossed into Switzerland, gave up our weapons, and were kept in an internment camp for the next three months."

"Three months?"

"We sat and suffered, while the armistice was signed, the Government retreated to Versailles, and the lunatics took control of Paris. At least, when I finally rejoined the army in May, I was in time to help drive them out."

"Why did you leave the army again?"

"To finish the job." Simon had become increasingly animated as he answered Boizillac's questions. Now there was a charge of venom in his voice. "We couldn't defeat the enemy from outside our borders.

But we have to deal with the enemy within. The street-fighting is over, but you and I know, captain, that some of the murderous scum are still hiding away. We can't let them escape." There was a fierce intensity in his eyes.

"Well, we must do what we can," Boizillac replied. "But much of our work is tedious – we cannot expect to flush someone out of hiding every day."

They reached the Rue de Rotterdam. Boizillac led the way to one of the town-houses that seemed to have escaped the damage that affected several of its neighbours. There was a gateway that gave on to an internal courtyard; an older woman was washing the grilles of the gate. She put down her cloth and eyed the visitors suspiciously.

"Madame Dubois?" Boizillac asked. "I am Boizillac, of the Paris police – and this is Simon." The younger man was a few paces behind him. "We received a letter from you."

"Good that you're here at last," she said, scowling. "Better if you'd got here yesterday. But too late to do anything about that, I suppose." She squeezed the cloth dry, over a bucket, and wiped her hands on her apron. "You see the staircase?" It opened on to the left-hand side of the courtyard. "Fifth floor. Door on your left. Monsieur et Madame Marchand, they call themselves. You can be sure that's not their real name."

"How long have they lived here?"

"Only since April. The apartment was occupied by a nice, older gentleman, but he left when the fighting against the Boche was over. Then these two moved in. Coming and going all hours of the night and day, until the end of May. Since then, it's like they're hiding away. He slips out maybe once or twice a day, but not her. I've seen her looking down into the courtyard, but that's all." She looked defiantly at her visitors. "If that's not suspicious, I don't know what is!"

"And when did you last see either of them?"

"Him I saw scuttle out yesterday evening. Didn't see him come back. As for the woman, she was peering round her curtains during the day yesterday. Haven't seen either of them today." There was a note of impatience in her voice. "Well, are you going to go up there?"

"We're on our way. Thank you." Boizillac remained to be convinced that Madame Dubois' suspicions had any solid basis, but the timing of the couple's stay in the apartment, and their behaviour, raised questions in his mind as well. He took the steps two at a time, though he noticed that Simon's progress was slower. "Come on, young man", he called. Simon moved more quickly.

They reached the fifth floor. Outside in the courtyard, the day had still felt fresh; here, under the roof of the building, the air hung with an oppressive warmth. However attentive the concierge might be to the entrance-gate, it seemed that she rarely cleaned the top of the building. Dust lay thick on the floorboards, cobwebs hung from the ceiling, and there was a smell that Boizillac associated with mice, or rats. He had seen worse, far worse, but this was a place where people lived through necessity, not choice.

He knocked on the door to the left of the staircase. There was no answer; the door swung inwards under the pressure. He pushed it half-open and called out: "Monsieur Marchand? Madame Marchand?" His shouts were met with silence. He turned to Simon. "We'll look inside. Even if they're not here, we may find something useful." The younger man nodded, without speaking.

It was a modest apartment. The door gave on to the living-room; it had a connecting door to a small ante-chamber which in turn opened into the bed-room. Each room had a window, above the courtyard below. As he walked through the apartment, Boizillac noted the simple wooden table and chairs in the living-room; the basin and jug on a stand in the ante-chamber; and the double bed in the third room.

And the body of a woman lying diagonally across the bed.

Though fully clothed, her dress was twisted and spotted with red stains. Her forehead was battered; her neck was bruised and raw; her eyes were open. She was dead.

Boizillac gathered his thoughts as he took in the scene. He guessed, from the stiffness of the woman's body, that she had died some hours before, perhaps the previous night. Seeing the disorder of the bed, sheets crumpled, pillows scattered, he felt sure that she had fought her attacker. She looked to be in her thirties, still young enough to offer a resistance which had not in the end saved her.

His gaze fell upon a cudgel that had rolled under the bed; there were traces of blood on it. It must have been used by the murderer; leaving it in the room suggested that he had left hurriedly.

"Is she dead?"

Boizillac had momentarily forgotten Simon, who hung back at the door to the bed-room. "She is. Hit over the head, and then strangled, from the look of it." He glanced at the younger man. "Have you seen a murder victim before?"

"I've seen worse than that on the battle-field." His voice was hard. "What do we do now? The woman's dead, and the man's disappeared."

"No, we won't learn anything from them. But this apartment may still tell us something. I'll search here. See if you can turn anything up in the living-room."

There was little enough for Boizillac to look through. To one side of the bed was a cheap wooden cupboard, which held a few items of clothing. He checked all of them, to no effect; the cupboard had no nooks or niches where anything could be hidden. There was a plain wooden chair in the corner, but that too held no secrets. The only other furniture in the room was the bed. He would rather have left the dead woman to rest where she lay; but that would be to neglect his duty. Using one hand to raise the mattress – carefully, so as not to disturb her position – he moved round the bed, sweeping with his other hand over the supporting slats.

His fingers fastened on a leather bag, placed centrally under the mattress. He retrieved it. Standing by the window, he opened the bag and took out the documents inside.

Simon came back into the room. "I haven't found anything." He sounded sullen.

"But I have." Boizillac held up the sheets of paper in his hand. "Correspondence." He looked through them. "Good God."

"What is it?"

"A note – no, two notes – signed by Charles Delescluze, and written just a month ago, in mid-May."

"Delescluze? The Robespierre of the Commune? What do they say?"

"One is to Marie Lalandin, and the other to Luc Mercier. Just two or three lines in each case, thanking them for their contribution to 'repatriating' the contents of Monsieur Thiers' mansion in the Place Saint-Georges." He turned to the younger man. "You know that Thiers' collection was pillaged by the Commune, and his house destroyed? Marie Lalandin and Luc Mercier must have been in the thick of it."

"So this is Lalandin?" Simon asked, nodding towards the dead woman.

Boizillac paused to read another document. "Yes. This is a letter from her mother, written only a week or so ago. 'Dear Marie – you tell me that you and the man Mercier have taken the name of Marchand while you stay in the city – I fear for you Marie – if you love your family, leave the city as soon as you can and come back to us'." He put the papers back into the bag. "Another grieving mother."

"But what about Mercier? A Communard, and a murderer. How do we find him?"

"We should find him, if we have patience, and good luck. But we can't be sure that he killed the woman."

Simon shot him a challenging look. "If Mercier didn't kill her, who did?"

"The Communards have many enemies. Someone else may have discovered the Marchands' true identity before us, and taken revenge for whatever reason. Perhaps it was Mercier, but we can't take that for granted. We must go back downstairs and tell Madame Dubois what has happened, and get her to close off this apartment. Then we'll arrange for Marie Lalandin's body to be taken to the morgue, and we'll spread the word about Luc Mercier." Simon nodded. "I'll take these papers with me." They left.

Chapter Four
Tuesday 13 June
Montmartre cemetery

A light rain was falling. Swathed in his great-coat, Luker paid it no heed, holding his umbrella closed at his side. He was no lover of graveyards; as often as he had needed to visit them over the years in the course of his investigations, he found them an uncomfortable reminder of his own eventual end. Three score years and ten. If he attained the span prescribed in the Bible... As he approached the cemetery, he cleared his mind of such introspection, and turned his thoughts to the task in hand.

It was eleven thirty. He planned to arrive early, to gain some sense of this site that he had not seen before, and to find a vantage-point where he could see the mourners before they saw him. He would then join them at the grave side, but a first, more distant impression would help him prepare to speak to Camille. If she appeared.

Some twenty minutes later, a simple hearse carriage appeared. A groom and a colleague, both in black livery walked, alongside the horse. Only a handful of people followed: a priest and two or three elderly individuals. Théodore Claudel, wearing a black frock-coat and a tall black hat, and leaning on his stick, was one of them; but there was no young woman there.

They reached a freshly opened pit. Luker trod slowly and quietly along the cemetery paths, and stopped only a few paces away. As the coffin was carried from the hearse and lowered into the ground, the party stood next to the priest, who spoke the prayers of blessing and valediction. "Show compassion to your people in their sorrow, oh Lord, and lift us from the darkness of our grief to the light of your presence." The mourners remained silent, heads bowed, until the priest made the sign of the cross over each of them, and moved off wordlessly.

Claudel made his way to Luker's side. "You came, as you said you would."

"I am glad that I did." He scanned the cemetery. "But Camille did not."

The rain had grown heavier. Claudel linked arms with Luker.

"Come now, at our time of life we cannot afford to stand around in this weather. Let us leave this place while we still can. There's a tavern not five minutes from here where we can find shelter, and something to eat and drink." Luker opened his umbrella above them, and slowly, locked awkwardly together, they stepped heavily along the puddling alley to make their exit.

As they entered the "Bouillon du Nord", it occurred to Luker that, if Stytche were with him, he would describe it as a "simple but honest stew 'ouse". Most of the customers were working-men, eating their bowls of thick broth with the same fixity of purpose that they brought to their trades. But the place was used to mourners seeking comfort after visiting the cemetery. There was a table just inside the door, next to the steamed-up windows. When Claudel and Luker came in and sat down, their sombre clothes still damp from the rain, no-one except the waiter gave them a second glance.

"A sad day," said Claudel. "I have known Jean-Pierre for twenty years, at least. A good neighbour, and a good friend." They gave their order to the waiter. "When did you last see Jean-Pierre, Mister Luker? I don't remember him talking about his English relatives."

The two men looked at each other. After a few seconds, Luker spoke. "I owe you an apology, Monsieur Claudel. My claim to be a relative was not true."

The other man tapped on the handle of the walking-stick that rested at his side. "If you are not a relative, Mister Luker, what are you? And why are you here?"

"I wish to be quite candid with you in my answers, but to do so I must trust in your discretion." He paused; Claudel said nothing, and kept his gaze firmly on the Englishman. "Well, I do trust you, Monsieur Claudel. I came to Paris..." The arrival of two bowls of broth interrupted his words. Once they had been set down on the table, he resumed, speaking more softly. "I came to Paris at the request of Georges Tisserand, who sought me out in London." Claudel raised his eye-brows. "You recognise the name?"

The other man took a spoonful of broth and swallowed it. Then: "A friend of Camille. Their friendship started some time ago, as these things do. But then, earlier this year, the two of them got involved in any manner of..." He chose not to finish his sentence. "I was very fond of Camille, as Jean-Pierre's daughter. I still am. But I did not approve of the Commune, or of what she and Monsieur Tisserand did for it."

"Georges Tisserand is concerned that she is in danger."

"Tisserand is right. A shame that he failed to persuade Camille to go with him." He took another spoonful. "Well, Mister Luker, I owe you an apology as well. I was sure that Camille would not be at her father's funeral today. I was with her when Jean-Pierre died, and she told me then, in tears, that she would leave within hours and go into hiding." He paused. "When and if she can move freely in Paris again, I know that she will visit her father's grave. But when that will be, I do not know."

"You will understand that Monsieur Tisserand feels that he cannot venture back to Paris at present. But he has asked me to find Camille and assist her in any way I can." He paused. "Have you any idea how I can find her?"

"You haven't touched your soup, Mister Luker. Save your voice for a moment or two, and eat." The Englishman obeyed. It was only as he ate the garbure and savoured the ham and cabbage that he realised how hungry he was. "Camille told me nothing about where she was going. Perhaps she didn't know herself." He leaned towards Luker. "Monsieur Tisserand might not be pleased to know that she had a companion when she went."

"A companion? Who was it?"

"I don't know. I stayed with her on the day that Jean-Pierre died, while she closed the house. It was evening when she left, and a man was waiting in the darkness to go with her. I saw little enough of him, though he looked older than Camille."

"Older?"

"Camille is thirty. The man could have been twenty years older. She waved me goodbye, and they were gone."

Luker rested his spoon in the bowl. "And she has not been back since then?"

Claudel shook his head. "Just as well. The day after she left, I saw a younger man prowling about the house in the evening. I can't say why, but I had a bad feeling about him. I saw him try the door, but when he found it was locked and the shutters were closed, he slipped away into the night." He sighed, wearily. "Bad times, Mister Luker, bad times."

"I am greatly in your debt for the information you have given me, Monsieur Claudel. It seems as though I have little hope of fulfilling the request which Georges Tisserand made of me."

There was silence for a few seconds, then Claudel spoke. "Do you have something to write with?"

"Why, yes, I have a note-book and pen." Luker fetched them out of his coat.

Claudel took the book from him and wrote in it. "Camille's closest friend. She may know more." He passed it back across the table.

"Thank you, Monsieur Claudel. I will treat this with the utmost confidence." Before closing the book and putting it away, he glanced quickly at what was written there: "Marie Lalandin, 43 Rue de Rotterdam."

They finished their meal. Claudel refused to allow Luker to pay for him. As they left, they shook hands and went their separate ways.

* * *

Tuesday 13 June
La Villette Abattoir

Boizillac and Simon had returned to their office, made arrangements for the body they had found to be transferred to the morgue, and written a first report of the incident. As was his custom, Boizillac stepped out briefly, taking his young companion with him, to eat lunch at a nearby tavern. Almost as soon as they got back to their desks, however, they pulled on their still damp coats and hats and headed out again. A sergent de ville had brought word of the discovery of another corpse, a dead man, carrying papers made out in the name of Marchand.

For the third time in two days, Boizillac made for the northeastern edge of the city. Not far from the docks stood the abattoir of La Villette, which the authorities had got back into operation as a priority once the fighting had ended. They passed the Rue de Rotterdam again, as they drew near to the giant buildings and entered through the gates that gave on to the site. The rain was sluicing off the roofs of the warehouse-like structures and washing across the surrounding yards.

Even through the downpour they could hear the sounds of the cattle in their pens, waiting for their turn to be butchered.

They stopped alongside one of the slaughterhouses. The sergent de ville who had travelled with them led the way to a side entrance. As they went inside, they could see lines of men wearing red-stained overalls, processing carcasses that swung from hooks above them. They were spotted by the overseer, who scuttled across to talk to them. A short man, he swung his arms back and forth as he walked.

"Japy," he said, curtly. "I supervise the work here." Boizillac responded by introducing himself and Simon. "Follow me." At the very back of the hall was a jumble of wooden boxes. One larger crate, big enough to hold a beef carcass, stood apart from the others. Japy pushed the lid to one side, to reveal the dead man, lying on his back. His front was drenched with blood, but it was his own, spilt from the wound inflicted by a knife whose handle could be seen, projecting from his chest.

Though the sergent had told them what to expect, Simon hung back a little: Boizillac wondered whether his experience of war had really prepared him for the shock of seeing death thrust into the midst of everyday civilian life. The overseer spoke up, with irritation in his voice. "We found him at the start of day, but not here. The body was outside, at the back of the building, under some old sacking. We brought him in here out of respect." He paused. "And to spare visitors the sight."

"And is this how you found him? On his back, with this knife in his front?"

"Just so. I got two of the men to take the crate outside, lift him in, and bring it back to here. The sooner you can get him away, the better."

"Is he known to you?"

"Never seen him before, and neither had the men. He had an envelope in his pocket, addressed to Marchand. Name means nothing to me."

"When do you start work?"

"Seven."

"So he was killed before then. When does the site close in the evening?"

"There's no-one on site after six."

"Is there a night watchman?"

Japy's brow clouded. "There ought to be, but we haven't yet replaced Germain. He stopped a bullet two weeks ago when he was rubbernecking near the barricades."

"Was he a Communard?" Simon asked.

Japy gave a snort of derision. "Germain? He was a fool!"

"We'll arrange for the body to be moved as soon as possible, Monsieur Japy. Is there any other information you can give us?" Japy shook his head. "You mentioned the envelope?" Japy looked at the sergent.

"I left that in the dead man's coat pocket. In case you wanted to see exactly how he was found."

Boizillac knelt down next to the crate. As he had already surmised, the knife, which had been driven upwards into the man's chest, had an unusually long blade, and several centimetres of metal stood proud of the wound. The man's hands were cut and bloodied, as though he had tried to pull the knife out of his flesh before collapsing. Boizillac folded back the man's coat on his left side, to reveal the pocket from which he withdrew the envelope. It bore the name "Marchand", and the address "Rue de Rotterdam". "Did you look inside the envelope?"

"No, sir," said the sergent. "I left that for you."

With some difficulty, Boizillac extracted a letter from the envelope: both bore traces of blood. He unfolded the paper: "Liberté, Égalité, Fraternité, ou la mort! The forces of reaction and their spies are everywhere. Come to the gates of the abattoir at La Villette at ten o'clock this evening. There is a way for you, and your woman, to escape the city. You will know me when you see me." He read the message out loud, then added: "No name given. But whoever wrote this knew the real identity of this man, and lured him here with the hope of escape."

"And you think it was a trick, and the writer killed Mercier?" asked Simon.

Japy broke in, impatiently. "Who is Mercier?"

Boizillac stood up again. "Luc Mercier was an active supporter of the Commune. We learnt this morning that he was living in the Rue de Rotterdam with a woman and that they had both assumed the name of Marchand. The woman was murdered last night. And so was

Mercier."

"How long will we be living in the shadow of this damned Commune? I rely on you, Monsieur de Boizillac, to ensure that this body is taken away with all possible speed, so that we can go about our lawful business again."

"It will be done, Monsieur Japy." Boizillac gestured to the sergent to put the lid back on the crate, took the envelope and letter with him, and led Simon from the building.

Chapter Five
Tuesday 13 June
Rue de Rotterdam

Luker was watching through the window as the cab carried him along the streets of the 19th arrondissement to the Rue de Rotterdam. It was early afternoon, but the darkened sky gave it the feel of evening. He had told the driver to take him along the length of the street before stopping. It was as well. Luker saw a sergent de ville standing just inside the gateway to number 43, trying to keep dry as he looked out into the roadway.

There was a church at the junction with the Rue de la Barrière. Luker climbed down, paid his fare, and hurried up the dozen or so steps to the shelter of the church's colonnaded façade. From here he could look back along the street, and gauge what was happening at the house that he hoped to visit.

He had not waited long when a simple waggon appeared: another sergent sat at the front, alongside the driver who controlled the pair of horses. The two policemen conferred briefly, then went inside the house, leaving the waggon stationed by the gate. Luker could see an older woman – the concierge, he presumed – waving her arms about as the men entered, then shouting at the driver, who seemed indifferent to her. After another short lapse of time, the men returned, struggling with a burden that they carried between them. The driver, rain streaming from his hat and coat, got down and helped them lift it into the back. He saw them place a thick cover over the waggon; the driver and his original passenger drove off again. The other policeman had a brief and agitated conversation with the concierge, then he too set off into the downpour.

Luker had clearly seen that their burden was the body of a dead woman. What was not clear was whether this was Marie Lalandin, Camille's friend, or Camille herself – or some third, unfortunate person.

He waited some time; then, opening his umbrella over his head, went down the steps again and walked slowly along the street. He would have to speak to the concierge. From what he had already seen of her, and from long experience over the years, he doubted that any approach based on simple curiosity would loosen her tongue. He would have to offer her money.

The gateway was ajar. He stepped inside and knocked at the door of the lodge. When Bernardette Dubois opened it, her ill-temper was all too apparent. Strands of grey hair hung over her face, which scowled at the visitor. Both her hands were clasped tightly around the handle of a broom which was tilted forwards, as though she might sweep any intruder off his feet and into the waste piled up in the courtyard. "Who are you?" she spat.

He had lowered his umbrella, and now inclined his head slightly: "My name is Octavius Luker."

She kept a hostile gaze fixed on him. "You're not from round here, are you? What do you want with me?"

"I am from England, Madame..?"

"England? Heaven help us both!" She tightened her grip on the broom-handle. "The last thing Bernardette Dubois needs today is a visitor from England!"

Luker offered an apologetic smile. "I came to Paris to see an old friend. It was only when I arrived here that I learnt of his death."

"There's been too many dying in this city recently," the woman remarked, acidly. "But what's it got to do with me?"

"My friend had a daughter, Camille, who has disappeared in the last few days. I understand that she was acquainted with a young woman who lives at this address. I was hoping that you might be able to give me some information to help me find Camille."

Madame Dubois' face took on an even more severe expression. "I'm sorry, monsieur, but I'm not here to help the world find its waifs and strays." She made as if to close the door.

Luker blocked the door with his foot, and drew out his wallet. "I fully understand your position, Madame Dubois, and I'm sure that you have a hundred and one tasks to complete today. But perhaps you would allow me to compensate you for, say, fifteen minutes' conversation? As a professional man, I know that time is money."

He had struck the right note. The concierge's attitude changed in an instant. "Fifteen minutes? Come in, then." She dragged him inside and shut the door at once. "We can talk in here." It was a small, dark room; there were obscure religious scenes hanging on the walls, and a crucifix stood on a table, which was flanked by two hard wooden chairs. "Sit down", she said, taking one of the chairs, but without releasing her hold on the broom. "You can put your money on the table, under the eyes of our dear Lord." Luker set two francs down. They disappeared at once into the pockets of the woman, who crossed herself, and gave her visitor a slightly less severe look.

"I was told that a woman named Marie Lalandin lived at this address."

Madame Dubois grunted dismissively. "She did. Only she called herself Madame Marchand. I didn't know her real name. But I thought that she and her man were bad 'uns. The police came this morning to check on them. Too late, as it happens." She paused. "The woman – they told me this morning she was really called Marie Lalandin – anyway, she was murdered last night. Can you imagine? I was down here, minding my own business, while someone was up on the fifth floor beating that woman to death!" She tamped the broom on the floor in emphasis.

"So Marie Lalandin is dead?" Luker asked, to encourage the concierge to continue.

"Yes, dead, her head bashed in. Can you believe it? Thank goodness, the police were here not half an hour ago and took her body away, to the morgue. Good riddance, I say. They were both up to no good."

"No good?" he repeated.

"Revolutionaries," she hissed. "Hiding away here, after spending the last few months turning Paris into a madhouse for layabouts and scroungers. Ha!"

"There were two of them?"

"Like I said, they pretended to be Monsieur and Madame Marchand. Last I saw of the man was yesterday evening, when he went out after dark. For all I know, he was the one who did for her."

"Is that what the police said?"

"The questions that the two who found her this morning put to me – they had no idea. I didn't expect much of the younger type, but the older one – Basilic, or Brasillé, some name like that – he should have had more of a clue. And as for the sergeant they left here on guard, he had the brains and manners of a half-wit!"

"It's been a trying day for you, Madame Dubois. I shall not

presume upon your time very much longer." The woman nodded, as if to confirm that he would indeed be shown the door at the end of the agreed fifteen minutes. "But I would like to ask you about Camille."

"Your dead friend's daughter? What was her full name – assuming it's a real one?"

"Camille Noiret. That is indeed the name with which she was born and raised. She has just turned thirty, an attractive young woman with chestnut-brown hair and brown eyes. Does that description sound familiar to you, Madame? Have you ever seen her visiting Marie Lalandin?"

She looked at him defiantly. "Is she a revolutionary as well?"

"I fear that in recent weeks she may have been drawn into the madhouse of the Commune, as you call it, Madame. But I have come here not to judge, but, in homage to my old friend, to find his daughter and to do what I can to help her."

There were a few moments of silence, while the woman considered his remarks. "I shall speak plainly, monsieur, that is my way. I'm no spring chicken any more, and you're even older, that's clear to see. It's no time of life to be chasing around after a wayward young woman. If I were you, I'd go back to London and forget about this quest of yours." She paused again. "But you won't, will you?"

Luker allowed himself a smile. "I'm quite sure that I am many years older than you, Madame. Old, and stuck in my ways. And so, yes, I do intend to continue with my quest."

"On your own head be it then." She tut-tutted loudly. "As to visitors, this Marchand couple had a whole procession of people coming to see them in April and May. I couldn't tell you how many, or what they looked like, except they were all much younger than me, and they all looked as though they'd got dressed in a hurry and without a mirror.

"You won't be surprised to hear that all changed at the end of May. No more groups of people laughing and shouting on the stairs. The two of them kept to their rooms, and the man only went out in the dark."

"And they had no visitors at all?"

"I didn't say that. They were few and far between. But there were a couple of women who came to visit in the last two or three weeks, sometimes separately, sometimes together."

"And did you see what these women looked like?"

"It wasn't easy, monsieur. They came here in the evening, and as often as not they wore shawls over their heads. One of them was blonde, with a pinched little face, and a limp. But the other one could well be who you're looking for. Brown hair, brown eyes, and a look about her which I don't doubt would appeal to men – young and old."

"That's most helpful, Madame. Has she been here recently?"

"I saw her two nights ago. She was with the Marchand woman for half an hour, or less, and then she rushed away." She shook her head. "She was with a man I hadn't seen before. They went off arm-in-arm. Can't imagine why she's taken up with him – he looked as though he was twice her age." She was silent for a few seconds. "And that's all I can tell you, monsieur – except that I still think you should know better than to go gallivanting about this city looking for some misguided young woman."

Luker stood up. "I thank you again, Madame Dubois. I appreciate your readiness to answer my questions on such a difficult day as this. I hope that the tribulations which you have suffered today will not repeat themselves."

"In the midst of life we are in death." She crossed herself, then advanced with her broom. "And in the middle of Paris we are surrounded by dust and dirt. I have my duties to do, monsieur, so I wish you good day." With no further ceremony she allowed him to leave, shut the door behind him, and disappeared inside the lodge.

The rain had eased. Luker found a cab to take him back to his hotel.

He had much to think about, but he found himself brooding on the name of the police officer that Madame Dubois had mentioned. Basilic? Was this the same police captain whose path he had crossed nearly twenty years before? Luker had been in Paris in 1852, and a witness to the police's investigation of the murder of an actress, apparently by Franklin Blake, the English gentleman. He still remembered the captain's name: it was Boizillac. If it was the same man, he would now be in his fifties, still pounding the streets in pursuit of assassins and villains. What had the concierge said: no time of life for such chases?

Luker shivered slightly, and pulled his greatcoat more tightly around him as the cab jolted along the streets.

Chapter Six
Tuesday 13 June
Pension Frensham

Octavius Luker had kept to his room for the latter part of the afternoon, glad to be out of the weather, and keen to reflect quietly on the events of the day. Thanks to his conversations with Théodore Claudel and Bernadette Dubois, he knew a good deal more about Camille Noiret's movements over the past few days; and, after his visit to 43 Rue de Rotterdam, he had a sharp sense of the fear which must be weighing on her mind. But none of this gave him any pointers to where she might be at present; and it was not obvious to him what more he could do to find this out. He needed to decide whether to return to London, and share what he had learnt with Tisserand.

He would take that decision in the morning. In the meantime, as evening fell, he made his way to the dining-room, for supper.

He was happy to dine alone. The first course was a consommé, far lighter than the broth he had eaten in Montmartre, but perfectly suited to drive off the last of the chill that he had felt from being in the rain. His bowl had been cleared, and he was awaiting a dish of wine-cooked chicken, when two more diners entered. One was Lewis Mardon. His companion was a woman, at least as tall as Mardon, dressed elegantly in black. Luker considered himself adept at judging the age of strangers, but at first glance he could not be sure whether the newcomer was in her late twenties or already past forty. Her pale, but attractive face had some of the softness of youth, but was marked by the shadows of experience.

Spotting Luker, Mardon spoke briefly to the woman and then advanced to his table. "Mister Luker, it is a pleasure to see you again. May I introduce Mrs Scales to you?"

Luker stood up and bowed briefly. "Are you also from England, Mrs Scales?"

"I am, sir, though it's some time since I last saw the country." She spoke curtly.

"Mrs Scales is also the proprietress of a pension here in Paris. She has accepted my invitation to dine here tonight, so that she might see the operation of another, albeit larger, establishment."

"Mister Mardon stayed briefly under my roof before deciding that he would be better served by the Pension Frensham." She pronounced these words with only the slightest of smiles, and did not disguise the tone of reproach in her voice.

Mardon flapped his arms. "Now, Mrs Scales, you have already forgiven me for that decision, which was motivated by the knowledge that I would encounter more of our country-men here." He turned to Luker. "Might I be so bold as to ask whether we might join you, Mister Luker, and take our supper in your company?"

"Well, if that is agreeable to Mrs Scales, I am very happy to share the table with you."

"I am obliged to you, Mister Luker", she said, as she allowed Mardon to pull back a chair for her to sit down. She glanced around the room. "There are few other diners here, and it will be good for us to join forces."

Mardon, also now seated, leaned towards Luker and said in a low voice: "I explained to Mrs Scales that Frensham's is going through the doldrums at present. Of course, the city's vicissitudes have played their part, but the sad truth, Mister Luker, is that the Frenshams lack the commercial acumen which Mrs Scales herself so effectively displays in the running of her own establishment." He nodded courteously towards the woman, then raised his voice again as the maid came to the table. "We shall be dining here as well tonight." Despite Mardon's protestations, they agreed that Luker's meal should be served at the same time as the others'.

"You must forgive me, Mister Luker. I have not seen you since our conversation yesterday morning. May I ask how you have fared since then? Were your efforts to find your relative successful?"

"I fear not. It transpires that he passed away last week. Indeed, I attended his burial ceremony this morning."

Mardon's face took on a pained expression. "I am very sorry to hear that, Mister Luker. It must be a grievous blow to you. Perhaps it was after all too importunate of us to intrude on your meal tonight."

"Not at all, Mister Mardon. Jean-Pierre was not a young man, and it was no great surprise to learn of his death."

"To die in a foreign country, at a time unknown to your family, must be a great sadness," Mrs Scales said, reflectively. She paused, as if struck by a memory, then spoke quickly again. "But did your relative live alone here in Paris?"

"No, he had a daughter, who was with him to the end." The food was brought to their table. Luker resumed. "Yes, a daughter. But I have not been able to see her."

Mardon held knife and fork stationary as he asked: "Was she not at her father's funeral?"

"She was not." Seeing the surprise on the other man's face, he went on: "She judged it better not to appear. A cause for regret on several counts, including the difficulty that I face in finding her."

"If she has gone missing, would it not be appropriate to seek the assistance of the police?"

Luker did not reply immediately, and then was pre-empted by the intervention of Mrs Scales, who remarked to Mardon: "In this city, at this time, there are many who may prefer to keep their whereabouts hidden, particularly from the police."

Luker glanced at her, and smiled fleetingly to acknowledge her insight. "That is so, Mrs Scales. And it may indeed be true of Jean-Pierre's daughter."

Mardon pondered the exchange as he raised his glass, swirled the wine it contained, and took a mouthful. "Then do you intend to return to England now?"

"I have all but made up my mind to do so. Unless you can counsel some other means by which I might find my way to Jean-Pierre's daughter."

While the two men had been served well-laden plates with their main course, the woman had chosen a simple omelette, which she ate with the deliberation of someone who took food as a necessity, not an enjoyment. "You could place notices in our newspapers, Mister Luker, or have bills stuck on boards and walls. But I suspect that such methods are not likely to commend themselves to you." He nodded his agreement. "Then you must let time take its course. The young woman you seek is of adult years?"

"She is thirty."

"Well, then, she knows her own mind. After the passage of time, and when the troubles that have disturbed this city in recent months have faded a little in people's memory, she may well choose to communicate again with her family. Unoriginal it may be, but I would counsel patience."

There was a conviction to her tone which suggested to Luker that she was drawing on her own experience. "It is unusual for one in his later years to be recommended patience by one so young, Mrs Scales." The compliment was acknowledged by no more than a slight raising of the eyebrows. "But there is truth in what you say. For the moment, my best course may indeed be to go back to London."

The rest of their meal was dominated by Mardon, who balanced the reserve of both Luker and Mrs Scales with his own ebullience, enthusiastically displaying his knowledge of the hotels and houses, grand or humble, of Paris. Luker was glad of the company, but Mardon's effusions did little to distract him from reflecting on his next course of action.

* * *

Place de l'Italie

For Lucien de Boizillac, the evening was not a sociable one. He had remained at the Caserne de la Cité until darkness began to fall, writing his reports for the day and looking through the correspondence, mainly letters of denunciation, which continued to arrive. Simon had gone, and the office had fallen silent, when Boizillac took his coat and hat and went out into the street.

It was nearly a week since he had returned to the capital. Nothing he had seen or heard since then made any reference to his missing brother-in-law. Boizillac decided that he had to go to where Marc lived. In all honesty, he could have found an earlier opportunity, but he had been reluctant to do so. For all that he promised his wife to find out what he could, he was in no hurry to discover what might be the fatal truth.

Marc Carreleur had worked on the rebuilding of many areas of Paris, and this included the housing around the Place de l'Italie, at the southern edge of the city. Some years before, he had bought a small plot of land there, hidden away from the main streets, and built himself a modest dwelling. Boizillac, with Laure and their son, had been there only two or three times; they had more often invited Carreleur to their apartment; but this was where Boizillac now headed.

He got down from the cab in the Place de l'Italie. It was a five-minute walk to the Impasse des Vieux Arbres, a dead-end which, as its name suggested, was overshadowed by a row of lime trees that had been in place long before the bricks and mortar of the Second Empire arrived. Carreleur's house stood under the swaying branches: a front, covered in fading plaster, showed a single window and door at street level, and one more casement above, under a lowering roof.

The shutters were closed; cobwebs had been spun around the door; leaves lay in heaps against the threshold, blown there by the wind. He knocked at the door, expecting no response; none came. The daylight was fading now, as he walked round to the back of the house. There was a small patch of grass here, around a willow-tree with shoots that reached almost to the rear wall: it was broken only by another door. That too was locked, and, though it was not leaf-obstructed like the front door, his knocking proved equally unproductive. He had no idea when Carreleur had last used the house, but it gave the impression of having been abandoned days, if not weeks, ago.

He walked back round to the front. Against the possibility that he would not find his brother-in-law in his lodging under the trees, Boizillac had brought a letter with him: "Marc – I am back in Paris – Laure remains in Châteauroux, with Marc-Antoine, but we are all concerned to know how you have fared – I ask you to get word to me – in person, if possible, otherwise by writing to me – if you need my help, I will gladly give it – in friendship – Lucien." The envelope containing the letter was in his coat pocket; he knelt down, and pushed it through the gap under the front door. He took one last look at the house, as it melted into the evening darkness, and left.

Chapter Seven
Wednesday 14 June
Pension Frensham

Luker had made up his mind to go back to London. He had breakfasted, completed his packing, and was settling his account at the reception desk. He felt a hand rest on his shoulder, and heard a voice say: "Mister Luker, I am glad to find you again."

He turned round, to see his companion from the previous day's visit to the cemetery at Montmartre. The man leaned on his walking-stick, looking flushed with exertion. "Why, Monsieur Claudel, I did not expect to encounter you here. Are you quite well?"

Claudel took the other man's arm. "A little fatigued by my journey here, but that will pass. I'm pleased that I remembered the name you gave me of your hotel, and that I arrived here in good time. Are you leaving?"

"I have decided to do so, yes. But come, we must find somewhere to sit down." There were a couple of chairs between the desk and the entrance-door. They settled down in them. "I travel back to London this morning since, for the moment, I see no way of advancing my search. But perhaps you have information that may bear upon my plans?"

Claudel leaned towards Luker, who mirrored the movement. "I was in my house yesterday evening. I was drinking a glass of wine, in honour of Jean-Pierre. I think I may have fallen asleep over it because, suddenly, I found I had company." He shook his head. "There is a side-door I never lock while I am in the house. Camille has used it in the past."

"She was with you last night?"

Claudel nodded. "She wanted to hear from me about the burial of her father." He sighed. "She shed a few tears. But she was glad that Jean-Pierre will now rest in peace." He paused. "I told her about you as well, Mister Luker."

"Of course. I thank you for that. How did she answer to it?"

Claudel's expression darkened. "Camille's mind is burdened by many concerns. She told me that one of her friends – the woman whose name I gave you, Mister Luker – was murdered in her apartment."

Luker lowered his voice. "I discovered that for myself. I went, yesterday afternoon, to the address that you gave me, and found the police taking away the dead woman's body. So Camille also knew about the killing when she visited you?"

"And it has made her even more anxious, and careful. I could not persuade her to trust you, Mister Luker, although I do so myself."

"But did you mention the name of Georges Tisserand?"

"I did, though I couldn't judge whether she was pleased to hear the name. All she would say was this. She will not trust any messenger from London unless that person is able to speak of secrets known only to Monsieur Tisserand and herself." He paused. "I came here today to tell you this, Mister Luker. If you can get such information from Tisserand, and convey it to Camille, then perhaps you can gain her confidence and help her to safety. But time is running short, I fear. She slipped out of my house into the darkness again last night, without saying where she was going. Who knows what dangers await her in the streets?"

Luker shook the other man's hand. "You are a good friend to her, Monsieur Claudel. My course is clear. I shall act with all possible speed. With luck, I should be back here in forty-eight hours. Your house will be my first port of call." The plan for the next two days had fallen into place in his mind. "But you have had a troubling time yourself. Let me arrange for you to have something to eat and drink."

Claudel waved a hand dismissively. "No, no. I've delayed your departure long enough. You have a long journey – a double journey – ahead of you. I have only to return to the Rue du Delta."

They got to their feet. The Englishman walked with Claudel as, leaning on his stick, he made his way out of the pension and into the street. Then Luker gathered up his baggage and headed for the Gare du Nord.

* * *

Thursday 15 June
La Villette

Wednesday had been without incident for Boizillac and Simon. But on Thursday, in response to a message from the dockmaster, they went again to La Villette. Fontaine, the dockmaster, ushered them into his office, where one of his workers stood guard next to a man who sat on a chair, with his hands and legs tied with lengths of rope.

"This little rat can't have been in the cellars when you searched them two or three days ago, but he holed up there last night. He stuck his nose out at the wrong time, so we grabbed him this morning."

Boizillac looked at the captive. He was a young man, in his twenties. The dirty, scuffed coat that he wore seemed several sizes too big; he was as thin as a rake, and the pallor of his emaciated face was emphasised by the black-framed glasses that he wore. He peered through the thick lenses at the new arrivals.

"What is your name?"

"I am Jacques Maigrelet. Who are you?"

"Boizillac, of the Paris police. And this is Simon. What were you doing in the cellars here?"

The man's head slumped, momentarily. "I just wanted somewhere to hide away and rest."

"Why hide away? Were you a supporter of the Commune?"

Maigrelet struggled on his seat. "Can I be untied? I need to wipe my glasses, to be able to see properly." Boizillac gestured that he should be released. The ropes were undone, and the man sat quietly, rubbing his wrists where the cords had chafed. He took off his glasses, pulled the flap of his shirt above his trousers, and cleaned the lenses on it.

Fontaine snorted with impatience. "How long is he going to sit there wasting our time?"

"Speak up now," Boizillac directed.

"Is it necessary for this audience to be present?" Maigrelet asked, indicating Fontaine and his worker. The dockmaster flushed and moved as if to strike the young man. Boizillac intervened.

"Monsieur Fontaine, you have done your duty in sending for us. We need not detain you longer. I trust you will allow us to conduct our interrogation in this office?"

"Well, you know your business. If it was left to me, I'd treat him the same way I treat any rat that crosses my path." He mimicked twisting a creature's neck. "Talk to him here, if you like, but I'd ask you to get him off these premises before the smell of him gets too strong for us." He took the worker with him and left.

"So, I ask you again, were you a supporter of the Commune?"

Maigrelet considered his words carefully. "I moved in the same circles as the Communards, but that doesn't mean I agreed with them."

Now Simon grunted scornfully. "Nor that you disagreed. Why else would you associate with them?"

"But it does mean that I know a lot about the Communards." Maigrelet's eyes peered through his glasses at Boizillac. He paused. "I can share that knowledge with you."

"The dockmaster called you a rat," Simon spat out. "And a rat you are."

Boizillac gestured to the younger man to ease off. "You followed the actions of the Commune since March?"

"Most of the time, yes. I attended many of their meetings, and stood alongside dozens of other supporters." He smiled ruefully, and rubbed his brow. "My head is full of their names, and where they lived. Surely that would be useful to you?"

"It might. But why would you give us such information?"

"If you see only a captured Communard in me, you'll arrest me and send me for trial, and I'll end my days in prison. But if you see me as a helper..."

"An informer!" Simon interrupted, contemptuously.

"...then it makes sense to keep me at liberty."

There was silence for several seconds. Simon's gaze switched back and forth between the two others, as he struggled to hold back the insults that were on the tip of his tongue. Boizillac weighed up what he had heard. "Our task is to bring offenders to justice, not to enable them to escape it. But, if you really do help us in that task, it may be that justice will treat you less harshly. I can say no more than that. What information can you give us?"

"A dead man was found at the abattoir, two days ago. It was Luc Mercier, who went under the name of Marchand. He was a dedicated Communard. He was murdered."

Simon started to intervene, but Boizillac signalled to him to wait. "Do you know who killed him?"

Maigrelet gave a hollow laugh. "The city is full of people who want to kill Communards. That's why I was hiding away here."

"We already knew about Mercier. What can you tell us about his associates?"

"He lived with a woman, Marie Lalandin, in the Rue de Rotterdam. She also uses the name of Marchand."

"Did you go to their apartment?"

"A few times, though not since the end of May. They often had meetings there."

"Meetings?"

"Marie Lalandin was one of a group of half a dozen women who worked with Courbet in the Federation of Artists. They helped to carry off Thiers' art collection when his house was ransacked, and then kept watch over it when it was stored in the basement of the Louvre. They called themselves the patrouilleuses."

"Not pétroleuses?" Simon asked. "The women who threw petrol on the fires that burnt in Paris?"

"Marie Lalandin and her friends? No, they were never fire-starters."

"And their names? Can you give us their names, and where they live?" asked Boizillac.

"Well, there was Louise Collet, and Nathalie Morelle as well." He paused. "But they didn't survive the fighting at the end of May. So two of the patrouilleuses are dead."

Simon's contempt for Maigrelet flared up again suddenly. His voice was thick with loathing as he spat out his words: "Three! Three are dead!"

Maigrelet looked at them blankly through his glasses. "Marie Lalandin was murdered two days ago. We found her body in the Rue de Rotterdam apartment," Boizillac said.

"Now you see why I wanted to hide," Maigrelet said.

"And what of the other women?"

"There were two more. One was Joséphine Rollin. I think that she was based over towards Clichy. The other was Camille Noiret. I remember her speaking of the Rue du Delta. But perhaps they're dead too now." His voice was hollow.

"And were there no men involved in this group? What did you do?" asked Boizillac. Simon's gaze was fixed on Maigrelet, who squirmed on the chair.

"I took messages between the group and the Hôtel de Ville, when it was necessary. And yes, there were other men. Luc Mercier, for one,

Marie Lalandin's partner. And Camille Noiret had a partner too, Georges Tisserand, but he fled the city at the end of May."

"Why did you stay here?" Simon asked.

"Tisserand had money, he could buy his way out. I have nothing except the clothes I am wearing. And the knowledge I have about the Communards."

The room was silent for a while. Simon's face showed the scorn he felt for Maigrelet, whose attention was however directed solely at Boizillac. The older man considered what he had been told, then spoke. "I'm sure you can tell us more than you have done so far. But we'll follow up the information about these two women, Joséphine Rollin and Camille Noiret. If it turns out to be accurate, I'll see what I can do to keep you out of court, for the moment." Relief spread across the other man's face. "But we shall lodge you in a police cell tonight."

"Does that mean food?"

"Basic food. Enough to stave off hunger."

"Thank God. I haven't had a proper meal in days."

Simon made a disapproving noise. Boizillac raised a hand to calm him, then spoke to Maigrelet: "Don't imagine it will be a lasting arrangement. But we'll keep you close at hand so that you can tell us what you know. What happens to you after a day or so remains to be seen."

Simon held the other man's left arm tightly as he got up, and the three of them left the office. After a final word with Fontaine, they left the docks and looked for a cab.

Chapter Eight
Thursday 15 June
London

Back in his office, waiting for his visitor, Octavius Luker fought against the weariness that he had felt since returning from Paris at a late hour the day before. Not for the first time, he uttered a prayer of thanks to the Metropolitan Police for parting company from Percival Stytche, who had kept the agency running during his absence, and who even now had set off across London to the address which Georges Tisserand had left with them.

He shuffled through the paperwork that Stytche had placed on his desk. There were Stytche's own notes on a case that he was pursuing, in the service of a warehouse-owner who suspected one of his workers of organising a series of thefts from his buildings. There was other correspondence, including a letter from a client of former years whose continuing doubts about his wife's fidelity had prompted him to seek assistance again. Luker could summon up no enthusiasm for raking over the same ashes again: unless Stytche wanted to take it on, he would write back to decline the case. There were a handful of bills to be paid, and some dreary leaflets from local churches and evangelical groups, desperately dreary and devoid of interest...

The sound of the street door opening jolted him from his sleep. He shook his head in self-reproach, stood up and took a few paces in the office, getting his thoughts in order. He opened the door on to the landing just as Stytche and another man came into view as they climbed the stairs.

"Here we are then, Mister Luker," said Stytche, brightly. "Monsieur Tisserand was even keener to get back here than me." He pronounced the name "Mon-Sewer Tissy-Rand."

"Thank you, Mister Stytche. Monsieur Tisserand, please come in."

"I'll be off out again," said Stytche, with a sly wink. "I have to see a man about a dog." It was the established routine whenever Luker planned a confidential meeting with a client. Stytche closed the office door, leaving the other two to their conversation.

Tisserand leaned forward on the chair where he sat, across the desk from Luker. "So, please tell me, did you find Camille in Paris? Did you speak to her?" His voice was agitated.

"Not yet, Monsieur Tisserand." His reply prompted the Frenchman to exclaim, and slump back in his chair. "Allow me to explain. I went to her house in the Rue du Delta on Monday. It was shut up and empty. But I was able to speak with a neighbour, Monsieur Claudel."

"Claudel? Yes, I know him. What did he tell you?"

"A good deal. He told me that Camille's father had died only a few days before. He told me that Camille had then closed the house and left. And he told me that her father was to be buried the next day."

"Did you go to the funeral? Was Camille not there?"

"Indeed, Monsieur Tisserand, I was at the cemetery in Montmartre on Tuesday and joined Monsieur Claudel to pay my respects to the deceased. But his daughter, Camille, did not appear. After the ceremony, however, Monsieur Claudel and I had further conversation. This time he told me that, when Camille left her house after her father had died, she was in the company of an older man."

"What?" Tisserand interrupted. "Who was this man?"

"I regret to say that Monsieur Claudel did not recognise him."

"And this is all that you can tell me, Mister Luker? That Camille has disappeared, with an older man whose identity is unknown?"

"One moment, Monsieur Tisserand. I have not finished my account." He gestured across to his desk to the younger man who had half-risen from his chair. "Yesterday, shortly before I left my hotel to return to London, Monsieur Claudel came to see me, unexpectedly. He told me that on Tuesday evening, when he was alone in his house, Camille came to see him."

"Thank God! So she is well?"

"It would appear so, yes. She wanted to know more about her father's funeral." He paused. "Monsieur Claudel told her about my inquiries, on your behalf. You will not be surprised to hear, Monsieur Tisserand, that events in Paris have disposed Mademoiselle Noiret to place her trust in strangers sparingly. She told Monsieur Claudel that she would deal with any messenger from London only – and I quote the words reported to me – if that person were able to speak of secrets known only to herself and to you."

The relief that had shown on the other man's face in hearing about Camille's visit to Claudel faded rapidly. "Secrets," he repeated, slowly.

He leaned back in his chair, and turned his gaze towards the floor. Luker sat in silence, leaving the other man to his thoughts. When Tisserand finally looked up again and started to speak, his voice was clogged and faltering. "There can be only one secret that Camille had in mind. I had sworn never to reveal it. But now it seems I must."

He reached inside his coat, retrieved his wallet, and took out from it a short length of red ribbon. He placed it reverentially on Luker's desk. "Soon after the siege began, we discovered that Camille was carrying a child, our child. We told no-one. Her father was already in poor health, and we wished to keep it from him. I wished to marry Camille, but she insisted on waiting until the siege was finished and we could lead normal lives again.

"And then, in January of this year, Camille herself became unwell, and miscarried. Somehow she still managed to hide her suffering from her father. But our child was lost, our daughter, to whom we gave the name Rubane, even though she never heard our voices.

"Camille had a ribbon in her hair on that day in January. We cut it in two. I have kept my half close to my heart ever since. Camille has the other half. This is the secret of which she spoke, Mister Luker. I have shared it with you, and no-one else. Guard it, I beg you, and use it only to gain Camille's trust."

There was silence in the room. Tisserand sat with his hand over his eyes. Slowly and carefully, Luker took a heavy, cream-coloured envelope from a desk-drawer, rested the ribbon in it, and sealed it up. He walked round to put his hand on the other man's shoulder. "I will take good care of the ribbon, I assure you."

"You will return to Paris?"

He resisted the fatigue that was summoned up by the thought of yet another journey across the Channel. The business was unfinished. "As soon as I can. And no later than tomorrow."

Tisserand got to his feet. "Whatever you can do for Camille, Mister Luker, I shall be profoundly obligated to you. Of course, you must let me know what I already owe you for your services." He made as if to fetch his wallet.

"There will be time enough for that when I have completed my work for you, Monsieur Tisserand," Luker said. "May I ask how you have fared here in London, in the week since last we met?"

"How I have fared? Well, to use an English phrase I have learned, I am still finding my feet. Auguste Rolandin has been most helpful. But I shall not be able to settle until I know more about Camille." The two men shook hands.

Luker showed his visitor to the door; and, even as he heard the footsteps descending the stairs, he turned his thoughts to planning his return to Paris.

Chapter Nine
Thursday 15 June
Paris

When Boizillac and his two companions had climbed into a cab at La Villette, his intention was to head straight back to the Caserne de la Cité. But he changed his mind after only a minute or two. Maigrelet was difficult to like, but Boizillac couldn't suppress a feeling of pity for the young man who, as he hugged his shabby coat close to his body, was clearly racked by hunger.

He stopped the cab near Place Lafayette, and they got out. Simon's antipathy towards Maigrelet had not abated; turning down the suggestion of a shared meal, he proposed instead that he should go to the Rue du Delta where the arrested man had said that Camille Noiret lived; it was only ten minutes' walk away. Boizillac agreed.

Now he and Maigrelet sat in "A La Bonne Table", a simple tavern tucked away down a side street. A bowl of soup was on the table in front of Maigrelet, which he spooned into his mouth with one hand while biting chunks off the rough-hewn bread that he held in the other. Boizillac himself had a small plate of cold meat and bread, and some wine.

"So, where have you been hiding for the past fortnight?" he asked.

Maigrelet waited until he had chewed through another mouthful, then looked across through his pebble glasses. "Mostly in the docks. Fontaine and his men walk about like elephants. You can hear them coming from the other side of the yard." He laughed.

"So why did they find you this morning?"

Another spoonful of soup was consumed. "Truth is, I was weak with hunger. I wasn't thinking straight, and stumbled out of hiding just as the elephants came past." He drew his hand across his mouth. "I'm surprised that Fontaine handed me over to you. I was half-expecting to be thrown into the dock basin." The soup was all but finished. He tore the bread into pieces and wiped the bowl clean with them. His gaze moved to the plate in front of Boizillac. "That looks good."

Boizillac pushed the plate across to him. "Here, have it. But I'm not sharing the wine."

Maigrelet wasted no time in clearing the plate. "I may regret asking, but why have you bought me this meal? Your young colleague doesn't approve."

"It's hard to think clearly with an empty stomach. Now that you've eaten, you should be able to come up with some more information that will help us."

"I'll do what I can. But there's not much more that I can say about the patrouilleuses. I don't know any more about what's become of Joséphine Rollin and Camille Noiret than I've already told you. But I wouldn't be surprised if Joséphine has fallen by the wayside – she was even skinnier than me, and walked with a limp as well."

It was hard to discern the eyes behind the pebble glasses, but Boizillac sensed that the younger man was telling the truth. During the time of the Commune, though, he must have rubbed shoulders with any number of other supporters. There was one in particular that Boizillac wanted to ask about, one who two decades before had also been an informant on the Government's opponents. "Tell me, do you know anything about a man called Marc Carreleur?" Maigrelet tilted his head sideways, questioningly. "About my age, medium height, balding."

"There are thousands of men like that in Paris."

"Carreleur is a builder, and has been constructing houses in the south and west of the city for the past fifteen years. I'm pretty sure that he used his expertise in the service of the Commune."

"Putting buildings up, rather than burning them down?" Maigrelet smiled weakly. "And the police want to bring him to justice for that?"

"You needn't concern yourself with why I want to find Carreleur," Boizillac said, impatiently. "But does his name mean nothing to you?"

The other man thought for a moment or two. "I do remember, a couple of times when I went to the Louvre to see the patrouilleuses, there were some men strengthening the basement walls. They were mostly my age, but one of them could have been the man you described. I didn't hear his name, but I remember seeing him talk to Camille Noiret. If you find her, perhaps she can tell you more."

"And when was this?"

"When was Thiers' house attacked? Mid-May? It was after that."

It was little enough, and hardly rock-solid identification; but for Boizillac it was at least half a pointer towards his brother-in-law, and one which Camille Noiret might be able to add to. He stood up from the table. "Well, I shall follow this up. The meal is finished. I'll take you to the cells now. But if you continue to help us, I'll see what I can do to help you."

With a last, regretful look at his empty plate, Maigrelet got up as well, and the two men left the tavern.

* * *

Simon quickly found his way to the Rue du Delta. Striding rapidly along the streets helped him dissipate the anger that he felt at the sight of Maigrelet, in his eyes a wastrel who had betrayed his country and now was prepared to betray his colleagues. Simon would not have humoured the man the way that Boizillac had. But there it was. And perhaps the information that Maigrelet had given them would prove reliable, and useful.

He walked the length of the Rue du Delta, carefully scanning the houses on either side, then took up a position at the junction with the Rue de Rochechouart from which he could watch any comings or goings. A couple of children were playing in the street: after a while their mother came out and fetched them back indoors. A housewife carried a bag of vegetables to another front door, let herself in and disappeared. An old man who had been trimming plants in his front garden straightened up, looked round, then stepped into his house.

Now the street was empty, its residents at their lunches. Simon walked back along it. Checking that the old man had not re-emerged, Simon went right up to the neighbouring house. Though it was the middle of the day, its shutters were closed, and it had an air of abandonment. He tried the front door, and was not surprised to find it locked; moving it backwards and forwards with the handle brought no-one to the door to see what was going on.

The other houses in the street all seemed to show signs of active residence. He had no doubt that this was the one where Camille Noiret had lived. Resisting the urge to force his way in there and then, he stepped out again into the street and made his way back to the Caserne de la Cité. He would have to report to Boizillac first, and then resume the chase.

Chapter Ten
Friday 16 June
Paris

Luker had travelled overnight again and, despite his best intentions, decided to postpone his further visit to Théodore Claudel until he had rested a while in his room at the Pension Frensham. And so it was that he made his way north through the city only in the early afternoon.

It was four days since his first visit; the Noiret's house had the same air of abandonment as before. He directed his steps towards the neighbouring house, and knocked on its door. It opened after a few seconds.

"It is you, Mister Luker. Come in." Claudel, walking-stick in hand, guided him into a small parlour room.

There were two dark and ageing arm-chairs: one, which looked towards the window on to the street, sagged indulgently towards the floor, and yielded further under Claudel's weight; opposite it, the other chair retained some of its original firmness; Luker sat down in it. Obscure pictures hung on the walls, and there was a shelf of skin-cracked books next to the hearth. One volume had been lying on Claudel's chair. As he put it to one side, he said: "Jules Verne's 'Journey to the Centre of the Earth'. Have you read it, Mister Luker?"

"I confess not."

"It's a favourite of mine. Reading it is more enjoyable than contemplating the world above ground. But no matter. I am pleased to see you again. How was your time in London?"

"I saw Monsieur Tisserand. I told him what Mademoiselle Noiret had said." He paused for a moment. "With great reluctance, he imparted to me the secret which it seemed to him must respond to her message. He confided in me that Mademoiselle Noiret was carrying a child last year, which she lost in January. And he gave me this." He took the red ribbon from his pocket, and held it out for the other man to see.

"Rubane." Claudel spoke the name softly. "A great sadness, which we kept from Jean-Pierre in his infirmity."

"We? You knew of this misfortune, Monsieur Claudel?"

"Camille managed to hide her suffering from her father and get to my house before the child miscarried. She stayed here the night after it happened. I told Jean-Pierre that she had fainted in my house, with a fever. She went back to her father the following morning, and carried on as though nothing had happened."

"I was concerned that I should have to reveal this episode to you, but it is clear that it was already known to you. Monsieur Tisserand said nothing to me about your assistance."

"Did he not? Well, he was here. But sadness, and shame, can make men act strangely."

There was silence in the room as the two men reflected on the memory that they had shared. Luker spoke again first. "I must ask, Monsieur Claudel, if my conveyance to you of this information will secure Mademoiselle Noiret's confidence in me, and if she will now allow me to speak directly to her. Do you expect her to visit you again soon?"

"There is no need, much as I would like to see her. We talked at length when she was last in this house. We agreed that, if you returned and told me what you have done, I should tell you where and when you can find Camille." Using his stick, he rose from his seat and went over to the book-shelf. Opening one of the volumes, he took out a folded sheet of paper and passed it to Luker. "The address is written there."

He walked to a low cabinet that stood in a corner of the room, and took out two small glasses and a stoppered bottle. He poured a measure of liquid into each glass, gave one to his visitor, and cradled the other one as he sat down again. "Let us drink to the success of your mission, Mister Luker, and to a happier future for this city and those who live here."

Luker carefully placed the folded paper in an inside pocket of his coat. The two men drank. It was an eau-de-vie, and Luker felt the warmth as it reached his stomach. "To a happier future," he repeated.

He was about to ask when he should seek out the address, but they suddenly heard voices outside and the sound of someone knocking at the door. "Just when I was enjoying this glass," the other man grumbled. "Carry on drinking yours, Mister Luker, while I see who this is."

Claudel went back into the hall and opened the front door. The start of the conversation which Luker overheard made him sit upright. "I am Lucien de Boizillac, and this is Emmanuel Simon, of the Paris police." Boizillac – that name again. So it must have been Boizillac who had questioned the concierge in the Rue de Rotterdam about the murder of Marie Lalandin only three days before; was it possible that this was indeed the same man who had investigated the Blake case so many years ago?

"I am Théodore Claudel." He spoke more formally than in his conversation with Luker, who detected a note of defiance in his words. "Why do you wish to speak to me?"

"We hope that you can help us, Monsieur Claudel," Boizillac continued. "We are trying to find Camille Noiret, and we know that the house next door belonged to her father. The house is closed up now. Can you tell us anything about Camille Noiret's whereabouts?"

"Why do you want to find Camille?"

"Because she was a Communard." The reply was shot back by a third voice; Luker assumed that it belonged to Boizillac's companion.

"We understand that Camille Noiret was one of a group of women who gave their support to the Commune." It was Boizillac's voice again. "In the last few days, other members of that group have been murdered. We want to find Camille Noiret to see if she can shed any light on these murders, and also, if necessary, to protect her in case she is also in danger."

"Surely anyone who supported the Commune is in danger now?" Claudel asked.

"Anyone who fought against the Government must be brought to justice, but that doesn't mean that they can be abandoned to private vendettas. Did you know Camille Noiret, Monsieur Claudel?"

"I knew her father, and so, yes, I knew her as well."

"And do you know where she is now?"

"Jean-Pierre Noiret died a week ago. His daughter shut up the house and left after the death. I cannot tell you where she went."

There was a pause in the conversation. Then: "We won't take up any more of your time. But if you see Camille Noiret again, or hear anything about her, do let us know as soon as possible." There was no reply from the householder. "Good afternoon, Monsieur Claudel."

"Good afternoon." The door closed, and Claudel walked back into the parlour, to find Luker standing to one side of the window and looking through it at the two departing figures. "Mister Luker?"

The Englishman took a last look through the pane and then returned to his seat. "Forgive me, but I thought that I might know your visitor."

"This Boizillac? You know him?"

"I do. It is many years ago that I was involved, here in Paris, in the case of a young English gentleman who became embroiled in the death of an actress. He was innocent of the crime, and was allowed to return to England. A friend of his, a Frenchman who lived here, was not so lucky. He was killed, soon after the actress died. It was Monsieur de Boizillac who investigated the case for the police."

"And you met him then?"

"Ah, I never spoke to him, but I was well aware of his inquiries, and I saw him give evidence at the trial of the English gentleman, which ended in his release from custody." Luker paused. "I have a good memory for faces. I was able to observe him just now as he left your house. It is the same man. Time has left its mark on his appearance, but it is he."

"I have not seen him before," Claudel remarked. "But this is not the first time that I have seen his companion."

"A younger man?"

"Yes. Younger, and less easy to deal with. There was an air of anger about him." He drank from his glass. "He has a very full moustache. I've seen his face before. I'm sure I caught sight of him out in the street yesterday, watching these houses."

"It may be that he was looking out for Camille, and when she didn't appear yesterday, he and Monsieur de Boizillac came back today to ask their questions."

Claudel looked pensive. "What a misfortune this Commune has been, for all of us." He shook his head, regretfully. "It would be as well if you could persuade Camille to leave Paris with you, Mister Luker. The police must do their job, of course, but the thought that they might arrest Camille and put her in prison is too dreadful to contemplate."

He leaned towards Luker. "You have her address. She said that, if you go there, you should do so in the evening, at half past ten. It will be dark then, but not so late that your appearance on the street will cause any surprise. You should make your way to the back of the house, and knock on the door, five times in quick succession, no more." He looked at the other man. "Is that clear?"

"Quite clear, Monsieur Claudel. I go to the house at ten-thirty, and knock five times on the back door. I shall follow these instructions to the letter."

"Thank you." Claudel fetched the bottle of eau-de-vie and refilled their glasses. They talked for a while about Luker's previous visits to France; then the Englishman took his leave and returned to the Pension Frensham, to await nightfall.

* * *

"You did well to identify Camille Noiret's house, Simon." The two men had reached the Rue de Rochechouart. They stopped at the junction. "So far, Maigrelet's information is proving reliable."

"Did you believe the old man?" The tone in which Simon asked the question made his own scepticism clear.

"Claudel? Not knowing where Camille Noiret is?" Boizillac looked back at Claudel's house. "It's possible. He may have had little to do with his neighbours. But even if he was on good terms with them, she may well have preferred to tell him nothing about where she was going."

There was a loose cobble-stone on the ground. Simon gave it a vicious kick, and it clattered across the road. "Or it's possible he knows where she is and won't tell us."

"Did you see anything suspicious when you were here yesterday afternoon?"

"No. But perhaps I wasn't here long enough." There was irritation in his voice. "And what about Joséphine Rollin? How are we going to track her down?"

"We have too little to go on from what Maigrelet has told us. I'm passing her name round the others at the Caserne, in case anyone else can provide a lead."

"How long will that take? We need to bring these criminals to justice as soon as possible!" His face was flushed.

Boizillac was struck by the intensity of his reaction. "It's good that you want to get the job done, Simon, but police work takes time. You shouldn't take it personally if we can't immediately find the Noiret woman, or Joséphine Rollin."

With difficulty, Simon suppressed his impatience. "So what do we do now?"

"We go back to our office and see whether we get any more information there. If not, there'll be other cases for us to pursue. We won't be idle, I'm sure."

They flagged down a cab and rode back to the Caserne, in silence. Boizillac could sense the frustration and anger weighing upon Simon's mind, but left his companion to brood. Youth was a two-edged sword: energy and commitment in spades, but a dearth of self-control and discretion. With luck, Simon would develop the latter qualities as the weeks went by.

Chapter Eleven
Friday 16 June
Pension Frensham

Luker had learnt over the decades that an ability to wait was an essential character trait for an investigation agent. Early evening had come. He had taken a seat in the dining-room and, as he looked over the menu, he recalled the French proverb: "La patience est amère, mais son fruit est doux" – the bitterness of waiting would bear sweet fruit.

"Why, Mister Luker." The greeting rang across the room as Lewis Mardon strode towards him. "I had thought you back in England."

"Mister Mardon, good evening. You thought aright. I was briefly in London since last we spoke, but have now returned, as you see."

The younger man took a tentative hold of the back of a chair at the table. "Might I join you, sir?"

It would be a good three hours until Luker needed to leave the hotel. He had no reason to rebuff Mardon; an interlude of harmless conversation with him could prove a pleasant diversion. "I would welcome your company."

A broad smile appeared on Mardon's face as he eagerly sat down. "I see that you are perusing the gastronomic possibilities. Might I suggest the dishes which are more successful?" Luker was happy to take his guidance, and they signalled to the maid who took their order.

"Forgive my curiosity, Mister Luker, but does your return to Paris signify that your search for your missing relative continues? And perhaps you now have greater hope of its success?"

Luker paused for a moment before replying. "You pose two questions, Mister Mardon. The answer to the first is certainly yes. When I was back in London, and tempted though I was to extend my stay there, I could not resist the prompting to redouble my efforts to find Jean-Pierre's daughter. As to your second question...hope springs eternal, and I bring it with me, to a city where hope has been in short supply."

"So you have not after all been swayed by the advice that Mrs Scales gave you, to wait until your relative decides of her own volition to communicate with the family again?"

The maid placed a bowl of onion soup in front of both men. "Those who have many years in front of them may perhaps find it easier to wait than others, like myself, who are nearer life's destination." He took a spoonful from his bowl while Mardon, smiling at the other man's remark, fell to eating his soup with gusto. "An impressive woman, Mrs Scales. Have you known her long?"

"Only a matter of weeks, Mister Luker." He paused as his spoon travelled back and forth between bowl and mouth. "I arrived here last month, and lodged for the first few days at Mrs Scales' hotel in the Rue Bréda." He lowered his voice. "It was a mistake on my part. Mrs Scales is a woman of impeccable character, I assure you. But the Rue Bréda has a very questionable reputation, and does not commend itself to our fellow countrymen when they come to Paris. As you know, Mister Luker, the Pension Frensham is a home from home for English visitors, and staying here has allowed me to gain the ear of no small number of them." He sat back, his bowl empty.

"If the area where Mrs Scales now has a hotel is so...questionable, why has she set herself up there?"

Mardon leaned forward and spoke softly again. "She never speaks of her past, but I have been given to understand that Mrs Scales first came to Paris some four or five years ago with her husband who then abandoned her; and that she fell ill and was cared for by a previous owner of her pension in the Rue Bréda, from whom Mrs Scales succeeded in buying the place on favourable terms." He waved to the maid to take away the bowls. "But, if I may make a slightly poetical comparison, to see Mrs Scales in the Rue Bréda is like spotting an English rose in a bed of thorns, and ugly French thorns at that. I have my own hopes, Mister Luker, and chief among them is that Mrs Scales will have the opportunity to acquire the Pension Frensham if and when the present owners decide to sell it."

"Is there some prospect of that?"

Mardon smiled. "I should not divulge my business secrets, Mister Luker, but I have a nose for these matters." He tapped the side of his nose as he spoke. "I can smell something in the air." The meat course arrived. "Ah, chicken with asparagus." He inhaled deeply. "A most agreeable smell too, though not the scent of commerce to which I was referring." A decanter of wine stood on the table. Mardon filled their glasses. "Let us drink to the realisation of our hopes, Mister Luker."

After a short interval, Mardon set down his knife and fork for a moment and asked: "You are no stranger to Paris, I think. Have you paid many visits here?"

"I have not kept a tally but, yes, I have often been here. Indeed, my visits seem to have followed the course taken by the Empire of Napoléon III. I was here at the time that he took the imperial title, I have seen Paris flourish and grow in the years since – and now I am back again, when the city that used to glitter and shine has been so overshadowed, by war and destruction." He sipped his wine, thoughtfully. "And the Emperor himself has meanwhile travelled in the opposite direction, to take up exile in Chislehurst."

"I am sure that Chislehurst is delightful," Mardon smiled as he responded. "But it is not Paris, and I have no doubt that this city will rise up again, very quickly. Why, the theatres are re-opening, the restaurants are offering the finest fare again, and Thomas Cook is already bringing our compatriots here to view the 'ruins of Paris'." He took several forkfuls of food in rapid succession. "How was the city twenty years ago, Mister Luker? My acquaintance with it is far more recent."

Luker took a while to compose his answer. "You bring me to reflect, Mister Mardon, in a way that I have not done before. But it seems to me that, while I have grown older in the last twenty years, Paris has become younger.

"When I first visited, it was full of dark corners and crooked little streets that were almost like the wrinkles on a man's face. All that changed under the Emperor: the darkness and the wrinkles vanished, the streets became bright, and smooth, and there was a new vigour about the place." He drank. "A city is not like a man."

Mardon's eyes sparkled. "If your meaning is that Paris is like a woman, Mister Luker, then let us chercher la femme!" He raised his glass again.

Luker copied his action, smiling. Mardon had the optimism of a man of thirty, and this was not the occasion to argue against it. Their conversation flowed freely to the end of the meal. Mardon departed, re-affirming his readiness to help his table companion find a house in Paris if he ever decided to settle there. Luker bade him good evening, and was left with an hour to prepare himself for his next attempt to meet the woman that Georges Tisserand had sent him to Paris to find.

Chapter Twelve
Friday 16 June
Rue du Delta

She was hungry and frightened, and struggling harder than usual to move her weaker, left leg in time with her right. Since she heard the news of Marie Lalandin's death, she had scarcely dared leave the wasteland shelter where she was hiding. But she could bear it no longer. She would go to Camille, and seek her help.

Darkness was falling as she reached the Rue de Delta. It seemed deserted, but she made her way falteringly, stopping both to look along the street and to rest her leg. Her heart sank as she reached Camille's house and realised that no-one was there. But she knew that there was a neighbour whom Camille had trusted, and whom she had briefly met once; and so, after a moment's hesitation, she knocked at his door.

Claudel had fallen asleep in a chair. It took him a while to clear his mind and come to the door. He opened it, lantern in hand. "Who's there?"

"Forgive me, sir, I'm a friend of Camille Noiret. Perhaps you remember me. I am Joséphine Rollin."

Claudel's irritation at being woken up faded as he saw the distressed condition of his visitor. "Yes, I do recall your face. Come in. It's too late at night for a conversation on the doorstep."

She came into the house, but, even as the door closed, she spoke again, rapidly. "I must find Camille. For the last week I've been keeping out of sight, waiting until I feel safe enough to go back to my rooms in Clichy. But I can't wait any longer. My only hope is that Camille can help me. Do you know where she is?"

"You were involved with Camille and the Commune?"

"I was. I helped look after the paintings in the Louvre, that was all. And now we are being hunted down, as though we tried to kill Monsieur Thiers."

He briefly rested his hand on her shoulder. "Stay there." He disappeared into the rooms beyond the entrance-way, and came back after a couple of minutes. "You can't remain in this house. The police called here this afternoon. Take this." He handed the woman a bag containing a chunk of bread and some cheese. "I can see that you haven't eaten recently." He put a scrap of paper into her hand as well. "And this is where you can find Camille. If you go there, give five knocks on the door at the back of the house. Understood?" She nodded. "Don't lose that paper. And now, for your sake and mine, I must ask you to leave."

"Thank you, sir," she said. In a moment, she was gone, limping back along the street. Claudel sighed deeply as he shut the door, and went to begin his night's sleep.

* * *

Place de l'Italie

He had timed his approach well. As he stepped down from the cab, it was twenty past ten. Through the windows of the taverns around the square, illuminated by lamps and candles, he could see drinkers talking and laughing. But his steps went the other way, into the deep shadows of the Impasse des Vieux Arbres. After only twenty paces, he was struck by how the noise and motion of the city had fallen away. It was a backwater that could easily be forgotten.

He reached the house under the lime trees: no lights showed, and the only sound came from the branches that swayed overhead. Following instructions, he walked to the back of the house, went up to the door, and knocked five times. A minute passed, then the door opened by no more than an arm's length. It was enough for a man to put his head round and beckon peremptorily to Luker. "Come in!"

He did so, and was confronted by two people. Immediately he recognised Camille Noiret: he saw the chestnut-brown eyes that had looked out at him from the portrait he had been shown in London, and the luxuriant brown hair which was tied up in a chignon. Her complexion lacked the freshness of her portrait, but this was the woman to whom Tisserand had lost his heart.

The man who was in front of her, shielding her, was clearly older: his grey hair and weathered face suggested to Luker that he was fifty at least. Powerfully built, grasping a cudgel in his right hand, he stood four-square, ready to meet any aggression with all the force that he could summon.

But it was Camille who now spoke. "You are the Englishman who went to see Théodore Claudel." It was a statement, more than a question. Luker reached into his pocket and produced the length of red ribbon that he had brought from London. There was a sadness in the woman's eyes as she stepped forward and took the ribbon from him. "Georges gave this to you?"

"He did. It is at his behest that I have come to Paris. My name is Octavius Luker."

There was a silence, broken when the other man spoke. "We should go downstairs." He took a lantern from where it had been placed on a small table and, as he raised it to shoulder-height, Luker could see that a flight of steps ran down from an opening in the floor, revealed by a trap-door that had been set back against the wall. Camille went first, followed by Luker and by the other man.

It was a spacious cellar, almost of the same dimensions as the rooms above ground. A table and four chairs stood in the middle, while at the back Luker could see a large store cupboard, holding a range of provisions. The cellar was divided by an internal wall that ran along its length; a door was half-open, and Luker made out a bed beyond.

"Sit down, Mister Luker," Camille said. They positioned themselves at the table. "This is Marc Carreleur. He has been good enough to shelter me since my father died – and since the death of Marie Lalandin." Pre-empting any question from Luker, she went on: "I don't suppose Georges will have mentioned Marc to you. So much has happened since Georges left Paris. Without Marc's help, I fear that I would already have been arrested by the police."

"I knew Georges Tisserand when he was still in the city," Carreleur said. "A young man of ability. It was better for him to flee. If only he had taken Camille with him."

The woman looked at him. "He wanted to, Marc. But I couldn't leave my father when Georges went."

"And now, Mademoiselle Noiret?"

Both men waited for her answer. "Georges has sent you to help me get to London, hasn't he?"

Luker nodded. "Yes. If you agree, I have papers which state that you have been living in London for some years, and clothes from an English dress-maker that bear out the truth of that statement."

"Go, Camille," Carreleur said. "We have seen what happens to others who stay here."

"But what about you, Marc? Will you come too?"

Carreleur shook his head. "No, I stay here. I'm as rooted in the soil of Paris as the old lime-trees outside. The trees will hide me while I bide my time. When their leaves come down this autumn, all this madness will have blown over. You needn't worry about me." He held Camille's hand for a moment. Then he looked across at Luker. "You are sure of your plan? You will bring Camille to safety?"

"I can be sure of my plan only when Mademoiselle Noiret and I set foot in London. But I have given it careful thought, and I shall leave nothing to chance."

They fell silent again. Their quiet reflection was abruptly broken by the sound of five knocks on the door above them. "Have you told anyone else about this place?" Carreleur demanded.

"Indeed not," Luker affirmed. "I have mentioned it to no-one."

"But it is the agreed signal. Claudel must have entrusted the secret to someone else," Camille said.

Carreleur stood up. "I'll go and see."

"I shall come with you," the woman said.

"No. You and Mister Luker stay here until I come back." He went up the stairs.

* * *

Rue du Delta

For all her circumspection, Joséphine Rollin failed to spot the man standing behind the gate of one of the houses opposite. As she limped towards the Rue de Rochechouart, he stepped out and strode determinedly after her. She paused at the junction of the two streets, unaware of her pursuer; but, as she moved off again, he caught up with her and seized her arm. She tried to break loose, but he was too strong.

"If you keep on struggling, I'll twist your arm behind your back until it's dislocated."

She gave up the attempt to free herself, and looked at her attacker. The man seemed her age; his most striking feature was his eyes, which glared down at her, over a bristling moustache. "Who are you?"

"Emmanuel Simon."

The name meant nothing to her. "Well, Emmanuel Simon, why have you assaulted me?"

"You are Joséphine Rollin, and you're a friend of Camille Noiret, aren't you? Where is she hiding?" She struggled against his grip again, and tried to conceal the paper that she was carrying. But Simon was too quick. He snatched the note from her and read it. "Impasse des Vieux Arbres. Thank you."

Rollin felt a sense of panic. She barged against Simon, pulled free of him, and tried to run away, tried to overcome her lameness. But it was no use. He was behind her at once; with his left hand, he grasped her neck; his right hand held a pistol, which he pushed into her ribs. "Enough of that!" he spat out. "We're going to this little hide-out, so that you can be reunited with your little anarchist friend. And if you don't do exactly what I say, you'll regret it dearly."

Her strength failed her. When Simon flagged down a cab, she climbed into it with him, and sank back, mute and in despair.

* * *

Impasse des Vieux Arbres

Carreleur opened the door only far enough for his challenge to be heard: "Who is it?"

Her assailant was twisting her arm behind her back again. In a failing voice, she said: "Joséphine. Joséphine Rollin."

Carreleur pushed the door back, and at once saw Simon lunging towards him. By instinct, Carreleur swung his cudgel towards the intruder, hitting his left shoulder. Even as he stumbled under the blow, Simon brought his pistol round and fired. The other man tried to swing the cudgel again, but a second shot from the gun hit him. Clutching his stomach, he fell heavily to the floor, as his blood drained from him.

Rollin stood in the open doorway, staring in horror. Simon seized her arm and pulled her inside, kicking the door shut. At the same moment, Camille Noiret came running up the stairs, calling: "Marc! What's happened?" She saw Carreleur lying on the floor, Simon with the pistol, and Rollin in his clutches. "Joséphine?"

"Forgive me, Camille! This man is a maniac."

"Don't waste your breath on hollow insults." Camille had bent over Carreleur; Simon pointed his gun at her. "Leave him, and go back downstairs. We'll follow." But her gaze was still fixed on Carreleur, and on the stain at his waist that was growing larger. "Do you want me to put another bullet in him? No? Then go downstairs!"

Luker had heard these exchanges. He was poised to follow Camille, but, hearing steps on the stairs, decided to hide in the cellar bedroom. Luker was no coward; but he had no doubt that, if he showed himself, he risked the same fate as Carreleur. He stayed hidden, quiet, and listening.

Simon forced the women to sit at the table. "Who are you?" Camille demanded.

"He says his name is Emmanuel Simon," Rollin said, wearily.

"You don't recognise the name?" he asked. "Didn't Nathalie ever mention me?"

"Nathalie? Nathalie Morelle? Why would she have mentioned you?" Camille asked.

His eyes blazed with anger. "A year ago we were engaged. But then, while I was fighting for France, and held captive in Switzerland, Nathalie fell in with you and the rest of the Communards, and got herself killed. For what? You call me a maniac, but the whole Commune was complete insanity. Idlers and layabouts pretending to run a city, but turning it into a madhouse. It all came crashing down, and took Nathalie with it."

His hand, still holding the pistol, shook with fury. "And just as she perished, so must you!"

"And Marie Lalandin?" Camille asked. "Did you decide that she had to perish too?"

"All of you, in your little group, you were all responsible for Nathalie's death. I found the Lalandin woman first, and got rid of her, and her man, Mercier. They put up a fight, but it did them no good." He stood opposite them and raised his pistol. He laughed briefly. "You've made it easy for me. No-one will hear any noise from this cellar."

Though he could only hear Simon, and not see him, Luker knew that he could wait no longer. He coughed deliberately. "Is there another rat hiding down here?" Simon said, contemptuously. He crossed to the door to the bedroom; but, even as he stepped through, Luker brought a small wooden chair crashing down on his head and shoulder. The pistol slipped from his grasp and ratted across the floor of the main room.

Luker tried to force his way past the other man. Simon seized him, but took hold only of his coat. They struggled, Luker attempting to get out of his coat, Simon grabbing at his throat. Luker broke free; but the younger man rushed after him.

Rollin acted even more quickly. She snatched the pistol from the floor, and pointed it at Simon. He swung towards her. "Give me that, you bitch!" he shouted. There was a shot; Rollin dropped the pistol; Simon put his hands to his chest, fell to his knees, and slumped forwards.

Chapter Thirteen
Friday 16 June
Impasse des Vieux Arbres

The sound of the gun-shot faded into a stunned silence. Rollin was shaking, but she slowly raised the pistol again. Luker had stopped in his tracks, and realised that she was pointing it at him. "Who are you?" she demanded.

"My name is Octavius Luker. I have come from London, at the request of Georges Tisserand, to help Mademoiselle Noiret escape." He returned her gaze, and added, simply: "I am a friend."

"Where is Camille?"

"She has gone upstairs. We should follow her." He did not wait, but climbed the stairs.

Camille was kneeling on the floor, cradling Carreleur's head in her hands. "He's dead," she spoke, softly. "Dead." At length she turned her gaze from Carreleur to Luker. "You are not hurt? And Joséphine?"

"We are both uninjured," he replied. The other woman appeared behind him. "And your attacker is dead as well."

Rollin knelt beside Camille and put an arm around her shoulder. "So Carreleur gave you shelter?" Camille nodded. "Was he also…"

"No. I have slept in his house this week, but not in his bed." There was a catch in her voice. "If he had asked, who knows? And now, he will never ask me, or any other woman." Rollin held her round the shoulders while she wept.

At last, she wiped her eyes and spoke again. "Did Georges tell you that you were coming to a place of such cruelty, Mister Luker?"

Luker remembered the sketches that Tisserand had shown him, of execution victims being thrown off the top of fortifications. "I was warned. I am shocked by the actions of this man Simon, but…I am not surprised." He paused. "I have seen your attacker before, earlier today." Both women looked at him. "When I was with Monsieur Claudel this afternoon, two police officers came to his door to inquire about you, Mademoiselle Noiret. One of them was Simon."

"What did Claudel tell them?"

"Very little. He denied any knowledge of where you were, and they went away."

"But he must have returned later to keep an eye on the house. He must have seen me go in and come out again, after I'd spoken to Claudel," Rollin said. "And that was when he ambushed me, and forced me to come here with him."

"Mademoiselle Noiret, I am sorry to press the matter again, but the events of this evening seem to me to make the case for your departure from this city all the more cogent." He turned to the other woman. "And for you to be accompanied by Mademoiselle Joséphine, as well. It is unthinkable that she should remain here, in these circumstances."

Camille looked down at the body of Carreleur for a few seconds, then spoke. "Well, there is nothing to keep me here any longer. I will – I must go along with your plan. Will you come with me, Joséphine?"

"And escape from this nightmare? Yes, yes of course."

"But I cannot leave Marc lying here on the floor. I must wash him, place him on a bed, and sit by him till morning."

"Is that wise?" Luker asked.

"Wise or not, I have to do it," she replied. "And it seems to me, from what Simon told us, that he has been acting for himself, out of some hatred that he has felt since Nathalie died. I don't expect any more callers tonight. But there is no need for you to share my vigil."

Luker hesitated. Then Rollin spoke: "I'll stay with you, Camille. We still have the man's pistol. I'm prepared to use it again."

"Is that agreed then, Mister Luker?" said Camille. "Joséphine and I will take care of Marc tonight. And we will wait for you to return here in the morning."

Luker was torn. Camille's own defender now lay dead; should he not stay with her in Carreleur's stead? But if he failed to return to his hotel, would that raise difficult questions? More importantly, if he delayed his return till the morning, would that not in turn set back the arrangements he had to make to get both women safely out of the city?

"Mister Luker? Joséphine and I survived the bloody weeks of the Commune's fall. We can survive one more night in this house. You don't need to stay here with us."

He made up his mind. "Very well. We are agreed. I shall go back to my hotel. In the morning, I shall finalise the preparations for the two of you to travel back to London with me, and then I shall return here to collect you."

There were no more words. Rollin let Luker out of the back door and, even as he left, Camille fetched a basin of water and a cloth, and knelt beside the body of Marc Carreleur.

* * *

Saturday 17 June

Luker wasted little time the following morning. After a rushed breakfast, when he was grateful not to see Lewis Mardon, he reserved a second room at the Pension Frensham, explaining that he was expecting visitors from London that day. Then he had one of his two valises brought down to the street where, after assuring the receptionist that he was not leaving but taking a present to a friend, he hailed a cab and was conveyed to the Impasse des Vieux Arbres. Struggling a little under the weight of the valise, he made his way to the back of Carreleur's house and knocked on the door, five times.

Camille admitted him. Her face was pale with fatigue, but she managed a brief smile to greet him. "We have done our duty, Mister Luker. Joséphine has fallen asleep, in a chair next to the bed where our friend lies. We are ready to take our leave of him." She noticed the case that he was carrying. "What is this?"

"I brought with me from London a simple, though I hope effective, disguise – a modest black cape and bonnet." He opened the valise. "If you wear this, it will lend you something of the air of an English woman." He paused. "But I brought only the one cape, of course."

"Then let Joséphine wear these. I brought my own cape with me when I joined Marc here, and I can tie some fabric around my hair instead of a bonnet. I'll wake Joséphine in a moment. But first, there is one more duty that must be undertaken on Marc's behalf. During the night, I remembered that, earlier this week, his brother-in-law came to the house and left a letter here, when no-one answered the door. Marc did not want to see him, but he wrote a reply, and was waiting until he thought it safe to deliver it. I have now written my own letter, to say that Marc has died, and included it in the same envelope. Can you ensure that the letters reach him, Mister Luker?"

He was keen to ensure as early a departure from Paris as possible; but there was no gainsaying the look of entreaty in her eyes. "I will attend to that."

She led him into the front room. He saw that Carreleur's body had been on a sofa; at first glance, he seemed to have fallen into the same sleep as had taken hold of Rollin, who rested on a chair next to him.

Camille gave an envelope to Luker. He read the name on the envelope twice, then spoke questioningly to the woman: "Lucien de Boizillac?"

"He is Marc's brother-in-law.

"But Monsieur de Boizillac is a police officer."

"Marc told me so. But he said that Lucien de Boizillac was a good man, and a good husband to his sister. How do you know of him?"

Luker spoke softly. "I told you that two police officers came to the house of Monsieur Claudel when I was there yesterday. One of them was Simon. The other was Monsieur de Boizillac."

There was silence. Camille spoke first. "I trust in Marc's opinion of his brother-in-law. I think that Boizillac cannot have known about Simon's intentions." She paused. "Even if he is a police officer, it is right that he receives Marc's letter, and learns of his death, and ensures that he is laid to rest properly." Her face darkened as she added: "And that he sees to the burial of the man downstairs as well."

"Of course." Luker placed the envelope inside his coat. "Rely on me to ensure that Monsieur de Boizillac is informed as you wish."

Their conversation woke Rollin. Camille quickly explained what Luker had told her. The two women went to another part of the house, taking with them the cape and hat that he had brought. Luker stood vigil, turning over in his mind what Camille had told him, and planning how best to get the envelope to Boizillac.

The women came back into the room, dressed to depart. Camille stood near Carreleur's body for a few moments. Tears filled her eyes; then she spoke. "He was a good man. It was his wish that I should leave. Let us do so." She held his hand for the last time, then turned away and left the house, with the others.

Luker hailed a cab, and they rode to the Pension Frensham. Their arrival went unremarked, and Luker saw them to the room which he had reserved for them. It was nearing the end of the morning, and he arranged that food should be brought to them. But he did not join them to eat. He had one last mission to complete in Paris.

Chapter Fourteen
Saturday 17 June
Caserne de la Cité

Boizillac had been puzzled that Simon failed to appear that morning. He had intended to go with the younger man and continue their inquiries in the northern streets and alleys of the city; but, when there was still no sign of Simon after an hour or more, Boizillac decided to stay in his office, sort through more letters of accusation, and prepare reports on what he had discovered.

Noon struck. He had spent long enough sitting at his desk. He left his office, went down the stairs and into the courtyard, then stepped out on to the Rue de la Cité. Glancing briefly across at the cathedral of Notre-Dame, he turned to his right and crossed the river to the Quai Saint-Michel. He was hungry, and he knew a family restaurant just five minutes' walk away where he could eat.

He failed to notice that, among the crowds strolling around the cathedral, an older man stood, watching the entrance to the Caserne; and he was unaware that the man was scurrying twenty paces behind him as he made his way towards the restaurant.

Luker had weighed up his options: he decided that he could rely only on himself to be certain that Boizillac received the letter with which Camille had entrusted him. There was a risk in making himself known to a man whose role was to track down the very people that Luker was helping. But his own instinct, reinforced by Camille's words, inclined him to discount the risk; and, if he were honest with himself, he had to acknowledge his wish finally to meet Monsieur de Boizillac, some twenty years after their paths had first crossed.

He couldn't match the other man's pace; before he could catch up with him, Boizillac had gone inside "La P'tite Maison". Luker had no other choice; he went into the brasserie as well. There were only a dozen tables, though the mirrored walls gave the impression of more. Looking round, he saw that Boizillac had taken a table at the back.

Luker approached him. "Monsieur de Boizillac?"

The other man looked up at him in some surprise. "I am Lucien de Boizillac. And your name, sir?"

"Octavius Luker." He stood by the table. "May I join you for a moment?"

Boizillac looked puzzled. "Forgive me, but have we met before?"

"We have not, Monsieur. I have the advantage, for which I apologise, of knowing your name though mine is unfamiliar to you." He paused. "If I may share your table, if only briefly, I can explain myself. And I act as well as a messenger."

"Then sit down, Mister Luker. Is that an English name?"

Luker sat down, still wearing his coat. "It is. I am here from London." A waiter brought a small carafe of wine and a plate of bread and cold meat for Boizillac. Luker waived ordering for himself. "But this is not my first visit to Paris. And on one of my visits, twenty years ago, I had some connection to a case which you investigated." He felt the keenness of the Frenchman's gaze upon him. "It was the murder of a young actress, for which Mister Franklin Blake was placed on trial."

"The English gentleman? He was released when the trial was aborted. You were a friend of Mister Blake?"

"I cannot claim that distinction. Do you recall that you received a letter which passed on information about the circumstances of the murder, noted by a young man, Louis Rougemont, who had played host to Mister Blake during his stay in this city? The letter was simply signed 'L'."

"I do recall that letter."

"It was I who wrote it, Monsieur de Boizillac. Though I failed to speak to you in person, nonetheless I knew of you, and of your work, at the time. Two decades later, we are both older men, but I am glad to have the chance to talk to you now."

The other man had been watching him closely throughout. "And was this the reason for you to follow me into this restaurant, Mister Luker? Surely not. You have more to tell me, I think, than a tale from half a lifetime ago."

The moment had come. Luker took the envelope from his pocket and placed it on the table. "I much regret it, but I am the bearer of bad news. This is a letter from your brother-in-law, written two or three days ago. But the envelope contains a second letter, written today by a friend of his, which explains that Monsieur Carreleur is dead."

Boizillac's face clouded. He broke open the envelope. It was Camille's message that he saw first:

"*Monsieur de Boizillac*

It saddens me greatly to have to tell you that Marc Carreleur died yesterday. He was shot, in his own house, by a young man called Emmanuel Simon. I understand that Simon was an officer in the Paris police, and that you knew him. Simon is dead as well.

Marc Carreleur was a fine man. He rallied to the Commune when it was set up, and used all his experience in its service, helping to make good damage to the city's buildings right up to the final days when the Versailles Army swept all before it. But Marc never used violence against anyone.

I knew him as a trusted colleague. After the fall of the Commune, and as the hunt for those involved became more intense, he offered me a refuge. For the last week, I have sheltered in his house, and it seemed as if this was one place where the hand of the Versailles Government would not reach.

Simon shattered that illusion. He forced his way in and shot Marc without warning.

I have tended to Marc, and left him lying peacefully in the house which he built. It must be for you to ensure that he goes to his final resting-place, with the dignity and love that he deserves.

You will also find Simon in the cellar: he lies where he fell.

I shall remember Marc for his kindness and decency. I shall grieve for him, as will you. I am sorry that his life was taken from him before you and he could meet again.

Camille Noiret, 17 June."

Boizillac stared at the letter for some while after he had read through it. Then he spoke, quietly: "Simon? Simon did this?" He looked at Luker, who nodded in confirmation. Boizillac folded up Camille's message and opened the letter that Carreleur had written.

"*Lucien*

I am sorry I did not see you when you called at my house. And I am sorry as well that you, and Laure, have not heard from me for many weeks.

I found a cause in the Commune in which I could believe. I lent it my support to help protect the city which has been my life.

Perhaps I should have foreseen how it would end. Death, fire, destruction. And despair.

I can no longer believe in a cause which delights in the killing of an Archbishop and his priests. And your belief in the established order, Lucien? Can you maintain it when its agents are taking so many of our fellow citizens and putting them to death?

Without our beliefs, what is important?

Ourselves, Lucien. My sister, Laure, Marc-Antoine, the son that you and Laure have raised – and you and me.

It cannot be long until I can move freely around the city again. And then we can be reunited, and make plans for the future. Plans that are free of beliefs.

Until then, in fraternity

Marc, 15 June."

At length, Boizillac lifted his eyes from the letter and spoke to Luker: "Have you read this?"

The other man shook his head. "Apart from yourself, only Mademoiselle Noiret has seen it."

Boizillac put both letters into the envelope, and placed it in a coat pocket. "Thank you for bringing it to me." He gathered his thoughts. "How is it that you were with Mademoiselle Noiret, at my brother-in-law's house?"

"I will be as honest with you as I can, Monsieur de Boizillac. I came to Paris on behalf of her fiancé who, unable to travel here himself, asked me to help her leave Paris. I must keep his name to myself."

"And did this man know that Marc was giving her shelter?"

"No. That I learnt from another source, about whom I can say no more."

Boizillac reflected for a moment. "So you were in the house when Simon got there? How did he discover the place?"

"Mademoiselle Noiret has a friend, Mademoiselle Rollin." Boizillac nodded as he heard the name. "It seems that Simon ambushed her as she was making her way to the house, and used her to trick his way in." He paused. "He shot your brother-in-law as soon as he opened the door. He intended to shoot the women too, but...there was a scuffle, and he was shot by a bullet from his own pistol, and died." Several seconds of silence elapsed.

"Simon claimed to be avenging the death of another woman,

Nathalie Morelle, by eliminating those with whom she had been linked during the Commune. He said that he and Mademoiselle Morelle were engaged, before he joined the Army."

Boizillac read through the letters again, and then asked: "Your task, to take Camille Noiret away from Paris...has it been accomplished?" As the Englishman hesitated, Boizillac spoke again: "No matter, Mister Luker. It is my sincere hope that you accomplish it. I shall not shadow you when you leave this restaurant. I must now go to the Impasse des Vieux Arbres."

"Here is the key." Camille had given it to Luker when they left the house, and he now set it on the table. "I can only repeat my regret over what has happened. I wish that I had made your acquaintance in happier circumstances."

They stood up, and shook hands. Without further ado, Boizillac left the restaurant and strode off determinedly. Luker followed more slowly, to return to the Pension Frensham. There was bright sunshine in the streets, but in their mind's eye both men saw only a dark cellar, and a shuttered room, where two lay dead.

Chapter Fifteen
Monday 19 June
London

Octavius Luker sat quietly in his office. If anyone called to seek his services, he would not turn them away, but he hoped that, today at least, he would be left in peace.

He thought back over the last days. In the event, bringing the two women back from Paris was uneventful. They had taken a cab from the Pension Frensham to the Gare du Nord; and, if anyone was observing the passengers boarding the train for the Channel, the appearance of an older man talking loudly in English to his two demurely dressed companions (albeit that they listened without speaking) must have dispelled any suspicions.

So, tired though they were when they finally reached London towards the end of Sunday morning, their nerves had been spared any further shocks. Luker had hoped to return on Saturday but, as a precaution, asked Stytche to stay in the office throughout the weekend; he used the camp bed that was stored there for such contingencies. When Luker and his companions arrived in Bethnal Green Cut, it was Stytche who once again went to fetch Georges Tisserand.

Luker, Stytche and Joséphine Rollin had waited outside the office when Tisserand went in to be reunited with Camille. A quick discussion between all of them followed, and it was agreed that Rollin should go with the other two to Tisserand's lodging. After many words of gratitude, they left.

Stytche had a meal brought to the office for Luker and himself; and, as they ate their pie and gravy, he heard the older man's account of all that had transpired after Luker had returned to Paris. "Good to see that lunatic didn't put any bullet-holes in you, Mister Luker!" he commented. At length, Stytche left as well; and, when Luker woke up an hour or so later, he too went back to his home.

Now it was Monday. There was a sheet of writing-paper on the desk in front of him; he dipped his pen in the ink-well:

*"Bethnal Green Cut, London
19 June 1871
Dear Monsieur de Boizillac
I hope that you will not object to my writing to you.
My decision to direct this letter to you has two grounds.
First, I wish to reiterate my condolences to you on the loss of your brother-in-law. The death of a relative or a friend is always a blow. How much heavier is the impact when the individual is taken from us in turbulent and unforeseen circumstances. I hope that you can find solace from knowing that Monsieur Carreleur lost his life in order to save others.
Secondly, if you will allow me, I wanted to set down my appreciation of the way in which you have discharged your professional duties. When we spoke in Paris, I recalled the contribution which you made to the extrication of Mister Franklin Blake from the web of suspicion that had placed him on trial for murder. I have little doubt that, without your intervention, Mister Blake would not have shaken off that suspicion and would have been sent to prison; if that had happened, I would have borne a heavy burden of responsibility for the injustice. It is thanks to you that my conscience is not weighed down by such a burden.
I must acknowledge as well that your reception of the news that I brought you at our recent meeting bespoke a particular understanding of the difficulties faced by others which might very well have been ignored by many in your position. I am doubly indebted to you.
I shall say no more, save that I would welcome it if our paths were to cross again. I hope that, if you ever find yourself in London, you would do me the honour of seeking me out, when we could perhaps talk at greater length. We have followed differing courses in our work, but my experience might be of interest to you, as I know that yours would be to me.
Please accept the expression of my deep respect.
Octavius Luker"*

He re-read the letter several times, and was finally satisfied with it. There was little prospect that he would himself travel to Paris again;

what he had now seen of the city, its ruined buildings and its troubled inhabitants, had robbed him of any desire to return. The realisation dismayed him, but his missive to Lucien de Boizillac softened the blow: even as he turned his back on Paris, he was glad to pay tribute to one of its citizens. He sealed the letter, and went out to send it off.

* * *

Friday 23 June
Paris

The coffin had been lowered into the ground, the words of valediction spoken, and the earth filled back in. Priest and grave-digger had gone; now three sombre figures remained, alone among the rows of burials in the cemetery. There was bright afternoon sunshine, but Lucien de Boizillac and his wife, Laure, felt a chill in their hearts. Only their son, Marc-Antoine, ran his finger around the tight collar of his shirt, and shifted uncomfortably on his feet. He was sixteen; this was the first funeral that he had attended.

It was five days since Boizillac had travelled to Châteauroux to tell Laure of the death of her brother, and to bring his family back to Paris. Though they had seen little of Carreleur in recent years, it was he, the older brother, who had brought Laure up after they lost their parents; the special place which he occupied in her heart was empty now; and she had gone through the motions of settling back into their apartment in Neuilly in a mechanical way, her thoughts elsewhere.

She linked arms with Boizillac on one side of her, and Marc-Antoine on the other. Looking at the newly dug grave, she spoke softly: "I shall miss him. Thank heavens that I have you two men to hold on to."

Her son fidgeted slightly, but did not try to release his arm. "Why did he die? Why have so many people been killed?"

Boizillac was not sure whether these were rhetorical questions. He, and Laure, had talked to Marc-Antoine about the uprisings in Paris and about the actions taken by the National Government to suppress them; but, even though their son knew what had happened, his understanding could not move beyond a sense of the pointlessness of it all. Boizillac paused, and then spoke.

"People die for their beliefs, Marc-Antoine. One side believes in the established order, which must be upheld; the other side believes in the rights of the ordinary people, which must be championed; both sides believe that the other is wrong. In the end, though, your uncle believed only in those who were nearest to him, like you and your mother, and me. And he died protecting such a person."

Laure was crying even as she held tightly to their arms. Marc-Antoine squeezed her hand. Boizillac's gaze moved from the broken soil, to the troubled faces of his wife and his son, across the sun-dappled monuments of the Montparnasse cemetery, to the jumbled buildings of the city beyond.

"Without our beliefs, what is important?" he said, quietly. "Ourselves."

Other Lucien de Boizillac Books

In *Coup de Tête*, Lucien de Boizillac begins his career in the Paris police. In November 1851, he, and his partner, Daniel Delourcq, are called upon to solve a series of murders carried out in the dark places of the city. The coup d'état which gives Louis-Napoléon the power to replace a republic by the Second Empire takes place in December 1851. Boizillac discovers the connections between the murders and the new masters of France, and is faced with a conflict of loyalties, between duty and family.

In *Coup de Pierre*, Boizillac is drawn into unravelling the murder of a young actress in the back room of a Paris tavern, in September 1852. The crime seems to have been committed by Franklin Blake, an English aristocrat (previously chronicled in "The Moonstone", by Wilkie Collins). Octavius Luker, an investigation agent from London, is instrumental in luring Blake to Paris, but passes information to Boizillac in an attempt to exonerate the Englishman. Boizillac's inquiries again reveal the hidden hand of the Bonapartist regime, which determines the fate of Franklin Blake.

In *Coup de Guerre*, Paris is pre-occupied with the Crimean War and the invasion in September 1854 of the Crimean Peninsula by allied French and British troops. A prominent advocate of the war is the Abbé Jean-Baptiste Charonnais, who uses his oratory to rally crowds in the capital behind the Imperial cause. But when Boizillac and Delourcq investigate a new series of murders, the trail leads towards the Abbé's household. A further and shocking killing makes clear the links between all the deaths.